Flawed Perfection

An Eve Sumptor Novel

Jourdyn Kelly

Copyright © 2013 by Jourdyn Kelly
Published by Jourdyn Kelly
All Rights Reserved.

No part of this book may be used or reproduced, scanned or distributed in any printed or electronic form without permission. Please do not participate in or encourage piracy of copyrighted materials in violation of the author's rights. Purchase only authorized editions.

This is a work of fiction. Names, characters, places and incidents either are the product of the author's imagination or are used fictitiously, and any resemblance to actual persons, living or dead, businesses, companies, events or locales is entirely coincidental.

ISBN Number—978-0615868455

Cover Art by: Jourdyn Kelly
Interior Design by: Angela McLaurin, Fictional Formats

Other books by Jourdyn Kelly
Something About Eve
Destined to Kill

NOTE:

Get to know Eve, Adam, and Lainey in depth by reading the prequel to *Flawed Perfection*, *Something About Eve*, first.

Table of Contents

Chapter One	1
Chapter Two	9
Chapter Three	27
Chapter Four	43
Chapter Five	53
Chapter Six	61
Chapter Seven	81
Chapter Eight	91
Chapter Nine	103
Chapter Ten	113
Chapter Eleven	123
Chapter Twelve	135

Chapter Thirteen	145
Chapter Fourteen	163
Chapter Fifteen	173
Chapter Sixteen	181
Chapter Seventeen	187
Chapter Eighteen	193
Chapter Nineteen	199
Chapter Twenty	207
Chapter Twenty-One	213
Chapter Twenty-Two	223
Epilogue	229
Acknowledgements	237
About the Author	239

Chapter One

Perfection. That's how Eve Sumptor-Riley thought of her life. She may be flawed, but everything else surrounding her is perfection. She thought of her marriage to the love of her life, Adam. Being with him was more amazing than she could have imagined. There was a time when she thought he would never be hers. Eve's past had stripped her of trust and emotion, and it was only when she met her best friend, Lainey, did she learn how to open herself up. She would never be able to thank Lainey enough for that gift.

Adam understood Eve's past. He understood her. Loved her. Even though Eve had always believed she was unlovable, Adam proves her wrong every day. The way he looks at her melts her heart and drives her crazy. The day she allowed Adam in, was one of the best days of her life—even considering what she went through to get there.

The birth of their daughter was the other best day in Eve's life. Eve smiled down at their baby girl, Bella, currently babbling and banging her toys on her activity walker. Bella's dark hair held the softest curls, and bounced as she tooled around the kitchen table. Her eyes, a combination of Eve's gray eyes and Adam's blue eyes, twinkled when she peered up at Eve. Bella is turning one in a few days, and Eve has been frantically trying to put together the best 1st birthday party ever. She doesn't really know why she's bothering with making it so elaborate. Bella won't know the difference anyway. But, your daughter only turns one once, Eve thought, and Bella is special.

"My two favorite girls," Adam said softly, bending down to kiss Bella on the top of her head. He then moved to Eve, kissing her lips lightly at first. When she moved in to him, he deepened the kiss, touching his tongue to hers.

"Yum," Eve murmured. The one thing about their relationship that has always been amazing is their sex life. And, Eve was completely happy that hasn't changed one bit, even after almost two years of marriage. In fact, it has only grown stronger. They had made love earlier that morning—one of Adam's favorite things to do since Eve let him stay—but even that wasn't enough for her.

"You look beautiful."

"So do you," Eve returned.

"You're the only one I will allow to call me beautiful," Adam quipped playfully.

"Stop," Eve chuckled. "You are beautiful." She couldn't think of any other word that would come close to describing him. His jet black hair, currently longer than he normally wears it—though you won't hear Eve complain, she loved running her fingers through it when they made love—framed a perfectly chiseled face that made the artist in her weep with joy. It also made the woman in her hotter than hell. The stubble across that sexy jaw rubbed her in all the right ways when he used his incredible, delectable mouth on her. And, the way he looked at her with those crystal blue eyes, could turn her into a sexual deviant at any given moment. And, honestly, with the way he looked in his navy pinstriped three-piece suit, and knowing all of the lines and muscle that lay beneath, that moment was coming fast.

"Hmm. What's on your agenda today?" She decided it was best to change the subject before her primal instinct took over.

Adam saw Eve's eyes darken and it took every ounce of will power he had not to take her right then and there. Their daughter was in the room, for crying out loud. He had more control than that. Though, if he were honest, not much more. Damn, she was the most gorgeous woman he had every laid eyes on in his life. How in the hell did he get so damned lucky as to land Eve Sumptor (now Riley)? She was perfection in the truest sense of the word. Her blonde hair was so soft and silky, he couldn't keep his hands out of it. Her face, God her face, with those striking gray eyes and full, pink lips could make him hard with just quirk of an eyebrow. And, her scent was intoxicating. So sensual, so purely Eve, it's a wonder he could concentrate on anything else when she's around.

"The bidding for Griffen Enterprises starts today." He grabbed a piece of buttered toast from the plate in front of her, stuffing his mouth before he lost his will power, and let lust take over. "This could be great for the company if I land this."

Eve knew Adam had spent hours upon hours drawing up plans for Griffen Enterprises, and they were spectacular. He is a magnificent architect. She should know since he designed her gallery and their home, and they were both perfect. Hell, they were more than she could've ever dreamed of, even being the artist she was. At their home in the suburbs—Eve told Lainey she could see herself here one day when she settled down—Adam had given Eve her own space to create art, develop photos and just lose herself. He made sure she and Bella had everything they needed, wanted and more.

"I've seen the plans, *amant*. You shouldn't have any trouble." Eve paused and smiled at Adam. "You're amazing, you know that?"

"You're just saying that so I'll build that extra room you've been wanting for your studio," he teased with another kiss.

Eve eyed Adam appraisingly. "Hmm. Do I need to compliment you for that? I thought a few sexual favors would do."

Adam sucked in a breath, and bent to kiss Eve yet again. He just couldn't keep his lips off of her. Damned waning will power.

"Well, now," he said between kisses. "Let me think about what you can do …"

"Hello? Oh!" Lainey stopped short when she walked into the kitchen, catching Adam and Eve kissing. She felt a small pang of jealousy, but shook it off immediately. "Sorry!"

Eve broke the kiss, reluctantly. "Lainey," she called before Lainey could walk out. "It's okay. Come on in."

"Please," Adam said. "I have to get going, anyway. See you tonight." He ran a thumb down Eve's cheek. "I love you."

"I love you, too." Eve grinned, knowing he was still getting used to hearing her say the words. She watched as he closed his eyes briefly and a smile touched his lips. Without another word, Adam kissed Bella on the head and Lainey on the cheek before leaving.

"I should know better than to just walk in," Lainey sat opposite of Eve at the table.

"You know you're welcome here anytime, Lainey." Eve smiled warmly at Lainey. She loves Adam with everything she is, but Lainey would always have a piece of her heart.

Lainey's smile was shy and knowing when she glanced quickly at Eve's mouth.

Eve reached over and touched Lainey's hand briefly, before turning back to her coffee and iPad. "Seriously, should it be this hard to plan a birthday party for a one year old?"

Lainey smirked. Seeing Eve as a mother was definitely entertaining. "You know, she's not going to remember any of this. You could just have a nice quiet day."

Eve raised her eyebrow. "Are you telling me that when Kevin or Darren turned one, you didn't hire acrobats and ponies?"

Lainey laughed. "I didn't go as far as acrobats and ponies, no." But, Eve was right. She did go overboard when her sons' first birthdays came around. "Just wait until she's a teenager."

Eve remembered Darren's thirteenth. The party Lainey threw for him didn't seem too overly done. It was simple and fun with friends, video games, pizza and cake. How hard could that possibly be.

"Boys are way easier," Lainey cautioned, reading Eve's mind.

"Awesome," Eve mumbled and rolled her shoulders to ease some of the tension.

Lainey cleared her throat, and changed the subject abruptly. The mere glimpse of Eve's cleavage—granted to her by Eve's customary three-buttons undone—was enough to have Lainey's mind reeling. "Are you ready to get to the gallery?" She rose from the table, and picked Bella up out of her activity walker.

Eve searched Lainey's face for any indication of discomfort or sadness, but for the first time since knowing her, Eve couldn't read the emotion on Lainey's beautiful features. Her dark blonde hair was pulled back, delicately, away from her face, giving Eve an unobstructed view of Lainey's alluring, green eyes. Her slightly bowed—and Eve remembered, very kissable mouth—was curved in a small smile as she cooed to Bella. Everything about her seemed happy and normal, but Eve couldn't shake the feeling that something was bothering her best—her only—friend.

"Lainey?"

Lainey shivered slightly at the sound of Eve's voice calling her name. It's silly to feel this way, Lainey thought, chastising herself. The two of them haven't been intimate since before the shooting, and she's been fine with that. Yes, of course, she has thought about Eve many times, but she has learned to compartmentalize it. For her sake as well as Eve's. She turned to Eve, avoiding looking directly into those amazing eyes.

"Yes?"

"Is everything alright?"

"Of course," Lainey answered, a little too brightly.

Eve sighed and reached out to take Bella.

"Hey there, baby girl. You ready to go to work with your Momma?" She glanced at Lainey, again. "If you want to talk, I'm here."

She didn't wait for an answer from Lainey. She didn't expect one since Lainey wasn't being particularly forthcoming. Instead, she walked out the front door, waiting for Lainey to follow, then locked it behind her.

Eve settled Bella into her car seat in the back of her Lexus LX 570.

"I sometimes miss your Jag," Lainey said softly.

"I still have it."

"I know, but you rarely drive it."

Somehow Eve didn't think they were actually discussing her sleek Jaguar.

"Lainey, just because I don't drive it as often, doesn't mean I don't think of it constantly."

"Hmm." It was Lainey's only response before turning up the radio. She lost herself, listening to P!nk urging her to try, try, try.

Chapter Two

"Oh thank God you're here, Mrs. Riley!"

"Mikey? What's wrong?"

Mikey has been with Eve since she reopened her gallery in New York. He began as her intern, but his extensive knowledge—and eagerness to learn more—prompted Eve to hire him on full time. She can't remember ever seeing him this flustered before.

"They are delivering the paintings today, including the Van Gogh's and Cezanne's. But, I don't think they're all here." He began going over the order form once more, hoping maybe he had just made a mistake.

"Give me Bella, Eve." Lainey reached over, plucking Bella from Eve's arms. "I'll take her to the nursery while you take care of this."

"Thank you." Eve turned her attention back to Mikey and the delivery men. She walked up to the stack of paintings leaning against the wall. She didn't need the order slip. Eve knew every painting, every print, every statue that goes in her gallery. This order was missing three.

"This is all you had in your warehouse?" She asked the deliverymen.

"Ma'am, we had everything, double checked. They were all there when we left the warehouse."

"Are you saying *I* did something with them?" Mikey shrieked.

"They're not saying that Mikey," Eve soothed. "Something happened between here and there, gentlemen. I paid a lot of money. I want my paintings." Her voice was gentle, but held undeniable power.

"Ma'am, we don't know what happened."

"Get your supervisor here. Let's figure this out."

She walked up to another stack of paintings laid out on the table as the men called their boss.

"Is everything okay?" Lainey stood next to Eve, watching her run her hands—and, oh, what expert hands they were—over the paintings.

"They're fake."

Eve's voice was so soft, Lainey almost didn't hear her. Even so, she couldn't have heard correctly.

"I'm sorry?"

She was startled a bit by Lainey's voice. She had been so focused on the paintings in front of her that she hadn't heard Lainey come up.

"The paintings. They're forgeries."

Lainey looked at the paintings. With degrees in Art History and Fine Art, she was proud of her knowledge. But, as she studied the art in front of her, she couldn't tell how Eve saw they were forgeries.

"How do you know?"

"The brushstrokes." Eve took Lainey's hand and gently guided her fingertips over the painting. "What do you feel?"

Besides you touching me? Lainey thought. "Um. It's smooth."

"Exactly. It shouldn't be. You should be able to feel each stroke, each line."

Lainey's hand burned where Eve touched her, but she refused to let it show.

Eve felt the heat radiating from Lainey and it confused her. She set that feeling aside for now, needing all of her focus to be on this screw up in front of her.

∞

"Ms. Sumptor?"

"Mrs. Sumptor-Riley." Eve corrected. The owner of the delivery company used to transport her paintings was a short, pudgy man with a round face, beady eyes and a razor thin mustache adorning thin lips. She felt an instant dislike towards him for some reason.

"Right. Well, let's see what we can do about your situation."

His condescending tone rubbed Eve the wrong way, but she held her anger in check.

"It isn't my situation, Mr. Branson. It is your problem to fix."

"Now, let's just hold on one second, young …"

"Do not finish that sentence, Mr. Branson." Her voice was cold, and the fury behind it was not subtle. "I paid millions of dollars for art. What you have brought me is not even worth the gas it took you to bring them here."

"Only three paintings are missing, Ms …"

"*Mrs.* Sumptor-Riley. And, the others are fakes."

"Impossible!" His indignant attitude and red face was almost enough to make Eve laugh.

"And, yet," Eve spread her hands to the framed art in front of her, "here we are."

"You must be mistaken. We'll take them to someone who can determine …"

"How dare you!" Lainey could tell Eve was holding back her anger, but she would not stand there and let this man belittle Eve's expertise. "Sumptor Galleries are the most prestigious galleries in the US. Eve is not only talented, but she is the most cultivated art dealer around."

Lainey's outburst didn't surprise Eve. She knew Lainey would always have her back. But, the fierceness behind it made Eve more determined to find out what was going on with Lainey. For now, Eve touched Lainey lightly, just a small run of her fingertips down the back of her arm as a thank you.

Lainey could feel the goosebumps form where Eve touched her, and it took all of her strength not to shiver in front of her and everyone else. Damn it. She thought she had been in control of these feelings.

"I didn't mean to insinuate …"

"Yes, you did, Mr. Branson." Eve was growing tired of his excuses and arrogance. "I want you to find my paintings. And, in the meantime, I will take the money you charged me for delivery. With how much you charge, you should be more careful."

"There is a strict no refund policy, Mrs. Sumptor-Riley."

Well, at least he got my name right.

"Mr. Branson, you *will* return my money. And, in light of what has happened here, I don't expect to be writing you any more checks." The statement was said with such finality that there would be no argument.

"I will get our investigators on it immediately," Mr. Branson grumbled.

"As will I."

"I don't think that will be necessary."

"You'll forgive my concern for your competency, Mr. Branson." Eve raised a brow, just waiting for a retort of any kind. When she received none, she went on. "I'll feel much better knowing my people are on it, as well."

Eve waited until they left before turning to Lainey. "Can I see you in my office, please?"

"I have things I need to take care ..."

"In my office. Now."

Eve turned on her heel and started up the stairs. She heard Mikey clear his throat and mumble something about sweeping the floor before the gallery opens.

"I don't appreciate you talking to me like that in front of Mikey." Lainey closed the door with an aggravated thud, standing just inside it with her hands on her hips.

"And, I don't appreciate you trying to avoid me," Eve shot back. "Something is wrong with you, and I want to know what it is."

"You have more important things to worry about, Eve."

Eve took two quick steps towards Lainey, effectively boxing her in with nowhere to go.

"*You* are important to me," she whispered harshly. "I don't like not knowing what's bothering you."

Lainey could feel her heart beating faster. "Give me some space. Please, Eve," she whispered when Eve didn't move.

Reluctantly, Eve backed away. "Are you and Jack having problems?"

Lainey sighed. "Jack and I are fine, Eve."

Eve searched Lainey's face for any indication of truth in the statement.

"Oh my God, Eve. I said we were fine. Do you think that's the only time I want *you*? When I'm having problems with my husband?"

"*You want me?*"

"Shit," Lainey muttered. She sure as hell didn't mean to say that out loud. Honesty is the best policy. Isn't that what they always say? "Yes. Does that really surprise you?"

"A little, yes. It's been almost two years and you've said nothing to me."

"I was trying to be a good friend. To you *and* Adam. But, I'm not like you, Eve. I'm sorry."

"What does that mean?" Even with the blood pounding in her ears, Eve heard the bite in Lainey's voice.

"It means I can't turn my feelings on and off like you."

"That's not fair, Lainey," Eve said, softly. "Do you think I don't think about you *every day*? About how it felt being with you?" Eve closed in again. "About how much guilt you felt, and the pain you felt? You couldn't even make love to your *husband*, which should have been easy and good for you, without feeling ashamed about it! We both made our choice that night I was shot. It was the right choice. I didn't turn off my feelings, Lainey."

The rational side of Lainey knew what Eve said was right. It was the damn irrational side that just didn't give a damn. She wanted Eve to feel what she was feeling. Maybe she just wanted to know that she wasn't going crazy.

"What do you want from me, Lainey?" Eve touched Lainey's cheek with a soft caress, and bent her head close. "Is it this?"

Eve's lips were a breath away from Lainey's. The anticipation spiked Lainey's adrenaline and her skin flushed. But, before they touched, Eve eased back with a frown.

"Can't do it, can you?" Lainey smiled mirthlessly.

"Don't dare me, Lainey."

"I'm not trying to dare you. I'm just saying the guilt isn't so easy."

Eve frowned again. "I was with Adam when we were together, Lainey. I know what guilt feels like."

"But, you weren't married to him. In fact, you broke up with him." Lainey reminded her.

"That doesn't mean I wasn't in love with him."

The words stung, but Lainey had always known Eve's true feelings for Adam. Even if Eve didn't.

Eve let out a frustrated grunt. "Tell me what to do, Lainey! What do you want?"

"I don't know!"

"What's going on with you and Jack?"

"Nothing! I told you we're fine! In fact, we're more than fine." Especially after I've dreamt of you, Lainey added silently.

"Then why?"

"It's this time of the year, Eve. This is when we ..."

Eve's eyes fluttered closed. "*I know.*"

"You remember?"

"I remember everything, Lainey." She pulled Lainey into her arms and just held her. "But, there has to be more. Tell me."

"I saw you," she confessed. "You told me you were working in your studio last night, so I thought I'd come by with a bottle of wine and talk."

"Oh, Lainey." Eve thought about the night before. It was Adam who surprised her in her studio. He made love to her, quite passionately, there amongst the art Eve created. It had been erotic and beautiful. She wondered—for a brief, inexplicable moment—how she would have felt knowing Lainey was there.

"I couldn't stop watching." Lainey lowered her eyes with shame. "I wanted to, my God I wanted to stop. But, watching you with Adam, all I could do was stand there and remember what it was like being the one with you. I'm sorry."

Lainey hiccupped a sob, and Eve tightened her arms around her. Eve pulled back, grasping Lainey's face in her hands. "Honey..."

"I should have called."

Eve knew firsthand how painful it was to watch. "I can't apologize for it happening, but I can be sorry that you saw that." Eve wiped a tear from Lainey's cheek. "You're wrong about me, Lainey. I can't turn my feelings off, but I can bury them deep enough to where they won't hurt anyone. I've had a lot of practice at that. But, I love you, Lainey. I will always love you," she admitted, softly.

The desire to kiss Lainey hit Eve hard, and the tremendous guilt she felt for that almost brought her to her knees. Before she could do either, her cell rang, shattering the moment to pieces. Recognizing the ringtone, she stepped back.

"Hi, gorgeous."

Lainey tried to make a break for it, not wanting to be this close to Eve while she spoke to her husband. Especially like that. But, Eve grabbed Lainey's arm and held her still.

Eve's voice was a husky whisper that never ceased to turn him on. Hell, let's be honest, everything about his wife turned him on. "Hey, beautiful. Are you busy?"

"Never too busy for you." She held Lainey's eyes as she spoke. It was stupid. She should have let Lainey go, instead of making her be a witness, but she wasn't done talking.

Adam cleared his throat. "You may want to stop talking like that since I have to be in a meeting in a few minutes and don't need a hard on when I get there."

Eve chuckled. "Sorry, baby. What's up?"

Blank. Adam's mind was completely blank. That's what she did to him. "Um. Oh! I called to tell you we got the account."

"That's fantastic! I didn't doubt it for a minute."

"I want to celebrate," Adam laughed. "Dinner, drinks … a little more."

"Just a little?"

"Ok, a lot more. I would like to invite Lainey and Jack."

"Just for dinner and drinks, right?" Eve teased. Adam's laughter rumbled through the phone, vibrating in her chest. Hearing him laugh was one of her favorite things. It was almost up there with hearing Bella laugh.

"You think I would let anyone else touch my woman?"

The tremendous guilt Eve felt earlier came back with a blowing crush, and she struggled to keep her voice light. "I'll ask about dinner."

"Thank you, beautiful. I have to get to this meeting now. I just wanted to share the news with you."

"I'm proud of you, *amant*."

"Thank you, Eve. That means a lot to me. See you tonight. I love you."

"I love you, too." Eve ended the call, and turned her attention back to Lainey.

"Now that you've completely ripped my heart out, can I go?" Lainey was seething.

"That wasn't my intention."

"Then what was, Eve? Making me listen to you speak like that to Adam after what we were just talking about was a shitty thing for you to do."

"I'm sorry. Lainey, I'm sorry. I wasn't done talking to you, and I thought if I let you go you would try avoiding me again."

"So, this was your alternative?"

Eve closed her eyes and took a breath. When she opened them, she saw Lainey staring at her with tears threatening.

"You're right. That was a shitty thing to do."

"Well, now that we're agreed, can I go?"

Eve dropped Lainey's arm, but stood her ground. "Adam got the Griffen account."

"That's really great." Lainey couldn't help but feel pride and happiness for Adam. He deserved this account after working so hard on it. "Tell him we said congratulations."

"You can tell him yourself. He invited you and Jack to dinner to celebrate."

"Shit. Now I feel like an even bigger ass."

Eve raised an eyebrow. It was a quirk that, with her wink, had somehow become almost a signature trademark for her, according to those around her. She didn't even realize she did it that much.

"I'm standing in his wife's office telling her I want her, and he's inviting me to dinner," Lainey explained to Eve's questioning look.

And, there was the desire again. Fighting tooth and nail against the guilt. Damn it.

"Will you come?"

Lainey studied Eve, wondering if the question was as full of innuendos as she imagined.

She decided no, there were no innuendos, just a question. "Yes, Jack and I would love to be there." She turned to leave Eve's office, only stopping when she felt Eve's soft hand on her arm.

"Are we okay?" Eve's voice was soft, almost pleading.

Lainey hesitated briefly. Were they okay? Could she keep her emotions in check? Does she really need more with Eve, and if she did and couldn't have it, could she live without Eve in her life at all? No. Lainey didn't believe she could.

She gave Eve a small smile, and touched Eve's cheek. "We're fine."

When Lainey walked out, Eve let go of the breath she didn't realize she was holding. Feeling even a sampling of the guilt that Lainey must've felt when she was with Eve, only strengthened Eve's determination to not put her through that again. She wouldn't be selfish this time. Or, was it this decision that made her selfish? Who the hell knew. All she really knew was that she didn't like the agonizing guilt she felt thinking of Adam when her lips were close to Lainey's. Whether she was doing it for Lainey or herself, it didn't matter.

Why do my problems come in multiples?

Pushing those thoughts aside, Eve sat down at her desk and picked up the phone. She'd be damned if she was going to let that idiot of a man Branson head the investigation of her missing art. She was surprised he was even clever enough to own the delivery service at all.

With a sigh, she punched the numbers into the phone and waited for the answer. She had no right to call him, especially after what he did for her two years ago.

"Hello?"

"James?"

"Ms. Sumptor?" His voice was filled with surprise. "No, wait, it's Mrs. Riley now."

Eve smiled, as she always did when she heard her name. "How about you just call me Eve. I think you deserve that much."

"Eve. I would ask how you've been, but I've been keeping track."

It was Eve's turn to be surprised. James was one of Tony's henchmen that turned on Tony to help Eve. When she asked him why he put his life on the line for her, he told her it was the right thing to do. He had just become a father then, and couldn't fathom how a man could treat his daughter the way Tony treated Eve. Perhaps he saw Eve as a daughter himself. He was older, though she didn't think he was nearly old enough to be her father. Maybe an older, protective brother. Whatever the reason, Eve owed this man her life. Still, the incident was two years ago. Why would he still be keeping tabs on her?

"Keeping track?"

He cleared his throat, obviously not meaning to divulge that bit of information. "Just making sure my efforts were worth it."

"And? Were they?"

"It would seem so. You're happy." It wasn't a question. "To what do I owe the pleasure of you contacting me?"

"I wish it were to just say hello." She felt rueful now, knowing that it mattered to him that she was happy. Eve never once followed up on how he was. It wasn't that she didn't care, or think about him. She just got busy living her life. A life without having to look over her shoulder.

"You don't have to feel guilty," he told her softly, somehow reading her thoughts. "If you need something, I'm there."

"I just need information, James, if you still have contacts."

"I do. What information are you looking for?"

"Have you heard of any art heists around the area lately?"

"Art heists?"

"Yes. High end. They would fetch millions on the black market."

"Have you been stolen from?"

"I have. A delivery that was made to my gallery today was missing three pieces. The ones that actually made it here are forgeries."

Eve was hoping he would say yes, that others were being stolen from as well. That would mean she wasn't a specific target. If the answer was no ... well, she would have to worry about that later.

"Hmm. I haven't heard anything."

Damn!

"However," he continued before Eve could respond. "I will keep my ear to the ground and see what I can find out."

"I would appreciate that. Is your account still active?" Eve asked, referring to the bank account she would funnel money into when he helped her before.

"There's no need for payment, Eve. It's just information."

"James, I owe you for way more."

"That debt has been paid."

Eve stayed silent for a moment. "I will wire $50,000 to the account," she said quietly. "If the information turns out to help me, I will wire more."

"Eve …"

"It's done, James. If you don't need it, or don't want to use it, then put it towards your son's education." She heard his sigh of resignation, and smiled.

"Thank you. I'll dig around and see what I can find out. Send me a list of your items, and I'll pass it around, see if I can't get your items back to you."

"Thank you."

"I'll be in touch."

With that, there was a click to disconnect that made Eve chuckle. James wasn't one for sweet goodbyes. He preferred to get to the job and be done. It was a quality Eve admired.

Alone now, and having done all she could do for now, Eve sat back in her chair, and studied the photos in front of her. Before Lainey, Eve's expansive, frosted glass and steel desk was bare of any mementos. Now, it held family photos that were more precious to her than the priceless paintings she held in the gallery.

A silver frame with Mickey Mouse cut-outs along the edge, held her first such photo. It was a gift that Lainey had given her after returning from their first vacation together. Eve had extremely fond memories of her time at Disney with Lainey, Kevin and Darren. She and Lainey had been lovers then, and even the boys had found their way into Eve's self-professed cold heart. Lainey had learned a lot about Eve during that trip, much to Eve's dismay. But, she couldn't regret any of what happened, because it brought her to where she is now.

She turned her attention to the next photo. Eve and Adam's wedding photo. Her dress was a modern, brilliant white satin and chiffon gown, adorned with crystal beads around her waist. If Adam's face was any indication when he saw her walking down the aisle, he loved the way the silhouette dress flattered her body. He confessed to her later that night in bed that it took all of his willpower not to march her out of there, and have his way with her before the ceremony even started. Eve knew exactly how he felt. When she saw him waiting for her at the altar, in his white tuxedo—beautifully contrasted by his black hair—her heart stuttered. And, her body reacted so intensely, she couldn't stop shaking until her hand was in his.

She continued inspecting the photos, coming across one of the entire Stanton family, that Eve had taken herself. She thought back to that day when she had Lainey, Kevin, Darren and Jack in her studio. Eve had actually been nervous having Jack there. The brief time they had spent together up until that point hadn't exactly been all that friendly. Jack had blamed Eve for a lot of the problems he and Lainey had. She couldn't entirely argue with that, given her relationship with Lainey, but she reminded herself that Lainey and Jack had problems before Eve came into their lives. Thankfully, the shoot had gone smoothly, and the relationship between Jack and Eve began to settle.

Eve picked up her favorite photo, and touched a finger to Bella's beautiful, chubby face. In the photo, Eve held Bella and Adam's arms wrapped around them both protectively and lovingly. Adam peered down at the two of them, while Eve hugged Bella close, and leaned her head on Adam's shoulder with her eyes closed in blissful happiness. The smiles on their faces clearly showed the joy and love they felt for each other and their baby girl. A small smile touched Eve's lips, thinking about the loves of her life. Her family. She went from having no one in her life, to being surrounded by incredible, loving people. It was almost more than she could conceive of.

For her entire life, she didn't believe she deserved love. The monstrous things her father made her do killed that hope for Eve. He had made her a whore—at least in her mind—and she didn't think she would ever be able to open herself up enough to let someone in. It was Lainey who showed Eve that she was, indeed, worthy of love. Even though Eve was involved with Adam, she kept had their relationship strictly physical. It killed her not to let him in, but she just didn't know how. Nightmares kept her from letting Adam sleep with her. Shame kept her from letting Adam love her enough to erase her past.

Eve found it easier to open up to Lainey. This was mainly because Lainey was married, and that made Lainey safe. This was also because Eve knew, deep in her heart, that Lainey was in love with her husband, Jack, despite the problems they were having. She knew it was selfish of her to take advantage of Lainey's situation, but Lainey was no less a willing participant. When the guilt started setting in for the both of them—not to mention their lives being on the line—they made the decisions that were best for them.

That brought them to where they are now, almost two years later. Eve, married to Adam with a daughter. Lainey and Jack doing well, their sons happy to have their parents not fighting anymore. They were happy. Or so that was what Eve thought before this morning when Lainey confused the hell out of her.

Again, she had to push that aside and focus on her work. James would find out what he could, and until then, Eve's life would go on. Adam's celebration dinner was going to be wonderful. This weekend, Bella's birthday celebration would be spectacular. She knew this because she would make it so. Eve was a self-made, successful woman. Despite her past, or perhaps because of it, she vowed to herself, to her mother—who was murdered by her father—that she would make something of herself.

Eve wasted no time doing just that. She owned restaurants and clubs, as well as some of the most prestigious art galleries in and out of the country. Now, with Bella and Adam, Eve had everything, and she would do anything she had to do to keep it.

Chapter Three

Eve stood just inside the door and waited for Adam. Bella has already been dropped off at Lainey's parents house with Kevin and Darren, Lainey was home with Jack getting ready for the night, and Eve opened a bottle of champagne and dressed—or rather undressed—for the occasion. She and Adam were going to start the celebration early.

Eve's lips twitched just thinking about what she wanted to do with Adam. To him. Her mouth watered, and she felt the arousal begin a slow burn in her stomach. She felt him near even before she heard the car door slam shut, and the slow burn became a fierce smolder. With two champagne glasses in hand, she turned up her mega-watt smile—the one that could make men drop to their knees—and waited with anticipation.

Adam turned the doorknob, feeling a sudden spike in his heartbeat. He only felt that spike when Eve was near. Just thinking about her, he felt a twinge in his dick. Damn, but that woman had a hold on him like no other. He had never felt passion like he felt with Eve. She was easily the best he's ever had. His wife—shit, he loved that—knew how to fuck, gave head like she was born to do it, and knew how to make sweet love that made a man feel as though he could die in her arms and be damn happy to do so.

He pushed open the door and nearly fell to his knees. Adam was greeted with the awe-inspiring vision of his wife in sexy as hell black lace lingerie, thigh-high, black stockings, a garter belt that begs him to use his teeth, and a pair of black fuck me pumps that turned the twinge in his dick to a full on, throbbing erection.

"Jesus, Eve," he growled. He dropped his briefcase and keys, not giving them another thought, and kicked the door closed before striding to her.

"Congratul..."

It was all she had time to get out before Adam's mouth crushed down on hers. His tongue plunged into her mouth, possessing her, caressing her tongue in a seductive way that had Eve's knees buckling. When he tore his mouth from hers to work his magic on his neck, Eve tried speaking again.

"I have champagne," she breathed.

"Fuck the champagne," he rumbled. "I have all I need right here." To emphasize his point, he moved his hand down to cup her between her legs. Then he changed tactics, grabbing her ass—her fucking perfect ass—lifting her until she wrapped her legs around his hips.

"Put the glasses down, baby," he commands softly in her ear. He walked her to the table near the door, waited for her to comply, then climbed the stairs to their bedroom.

Eve has always needed some sort of consistency in her life. For her, this came in the form of similarly decorated master bedrooms in each of the properties they owned. Everything from white carpets and linen—Eve's signature color—to the platform bed as big as an ocean in the middle of the room. He walked up that platform, and released Eve until she stood before him.

"How long do we have?"

"Long enough to get the celebration going." Eve reached for Adam's tie, loosening it and sliding it from his neck. "Not long enough to do everything I want to do to you," she whispered against his lips.

"Fuck." His cock was jumping. Throbbing. The need for Eve was almost excruciating. She was unbuttoning his shirt, and he left her to it as he let his hands roam her toned, sensual body. His hands engulfed her swollen breasts. They were slightly bigger now after she had Bella, and Adam certainly wasn't complaining. He dipped his head to taste her, slipping her nipple into his mouth, sucking. Biting. Her murmurs of pleasure washed over him as she slides his shirt off his shoulders. He wanted to continue his journey down her body, but she stopped him.

"No, *amant*. This is to celebrate your accomplishment."

"That's what I'm trying to do, beautiful."

Eve smiled, that beautiful, gut-wrenching smile, and worked his belt. She turned them until Adam's back was to the bed. Unbuttoning his pants, she let them fall to his feet, along with his boxer briefs, then nudged him until he sat on the bed. Eve got to her knees in front of him, grasping his cock in her hand.

"I love that I do this to you." She stroked him as she looked into his eyes. He groaned, moving his hips to the rhythm of her hand. She tipped her head, using her tongue to stroke him this time. Adam's head fell back in complete ecstasy feeling her hot tongue roll over him. When she took him into her mouth, he fisted his hand into her hair, guiding the bobbing of her head.

"That feels good, baby."

Her answering moan vibrated against his cock, sending a thrill right through to his core. She sucked him like it was her favorite thing to do, and right at this moment, he believed it was.

God he felt good in her mouth. Tasted even better. Eve couldn't get enough of him. He was smooth as velvet, and so hard her sex ached to have him inside her, but she continued working him with her mouth. He was huge, much more than she could handle with her mouth alone, so she used her hands to help her while taking him as far down her throat as she could. She came back up, hollowing her cheeks as she sucked, then rolled her tongue around the tip of his cock, reveling in the taste of him. Eve felt his body tense as she pulled the bulging head into her mouth, stroking him at the same time.

"Eve." His voice was hoarse and strained, and Eve knew he was close. "Baby, do you want me to come in your mouth?"

"Mmhmm." Eve sucked harder, stroked faster, wanting to feel his orgasm in her mouth. She loved the taste of him. Needed it. On a pleasured groan, she felt his body jerk as he came. The warmth of him coated her throat, and she swallowed instinctively, trying to keep up. Using her finger, she wiped the bit of Adam's semen that trickled from her mouth, and sucked it from her finger while he watched.

"Damn, beautiful, you undo me." He ran his fingers through her silky hair, and she smiled up at him.

"Good."

Eve rose from her knees, and straddled him on the bed.

"You taste amazing, baby."

"My turn?"

"Unh uh. We have to get ready to go."

Adam's voice was rough when he muttered, "When I get you home tonight ..." trailing off as he stood with Eve still wrapped around him.

Eve laughed softly. "Can't wait."

Dinner that night was at Eve's restaurant, The Garden of Eve, and the evening couldn't have gone better. Lainey seemed to be in good spirits. Whether she was pretending or not, Eve didn't know. If it was an act, Eve appreciated the effort Lainey put in for Adam's sake.

After dinner, Adam made good on his promise to continue the amazing beginning to their celebration. To say that she felt the earth move wasn't an exaggeration in the least. The things that man could do to her made Eve's toes curl, her heart skip and her brain turn to mush. Needless to say, her mood was exceptionally good when she woke up the next morning. The morning shower sex only made it that much better.

It wasn't until Eve and Lainey were driving to the gallery that she found out Lainey's good mood was a farce the evening before.

"You couldn't have waited until after dinner to fuck Adam?"

Eve sighed and glanced in the mirror at Bella who was sleeping in her car seat behind her. Lainey's harsh words were whispered, but Eve certainly heard them loud and clear.

"Lainey ..."

"You *know* how I feel, you *know* I've been struggling. Did you really think I wouldn't notice?"

"You're being unreasonable."

"*Unreasonable?*" Lainey hissed.

"Yes, unreasonable." Eve was trying to keep her tone even and calm, but it was seriously taking a lot of will power to do so.

"You couldn't have controlled yourself for a few hours for my sake?"

That was it. Eve could no longer restrain her fury. She pulled over to the side of the road, jerking to a stop and turned to Lainey. Her arm draped over the back of the seat, and she gripped Lainey's headrest in a white-knuckle grip.

"How dare you?" She was fuming. "How dare you make me feel guilty about being with my husband?"

"I just thought you would be a little more sensitive to our situation. Instead, you have sex before our dinner together. Then I have to watch you two …"

"Enough! I can't believe you're doing this to me, Lainey. Yet, here we are. So, fine, you want to do this, let's do it. First of all, Adam and I didn't have sex before dinner, I sucked him off. We saved the mind-boggling, earth-moving *fucking* for *after* dinner."

Lainey flinched, and Eve was instantly sorry for being so blunt, but she told herself it was Lainey's own fault for doing this to her.

"I have never once, not even when I was *forced* to watch you fucking Jack, made you feel guilty about it. In fact, I *encouraged* you to be with him! I told you *every single time* that it was natural and right!" She leaned in, holding Lainey's hurt stare before continuing. "And *every* time I was with Adam you made me feel guilty about it." She whispered.

"Eve ..."

"No! I'm done, Lainey. I'm through with feeling guilty about fucking my *husband*! You're not being fair. I didn't *make* you watch us in my studio! I didn't *hide* you in the closet!"

Lainey cringed at the memory of Eve hiding in closet as Lainey and Jack made love. Or, more accurately, when Jack had his fun and left Lainey wanting, no, needing more. It was a regret Lainey holds to this day. Of course, she didn't plan for that to happen. Eve had been there with her trying to help Lainey seduce Jack. Trying to help Lainey fix her marriage. Then, when Jack came home earlier than expected, Eve was forced to hide. It tore Lainey's heart out when she saw the hurt in Eve's eyes as she watched. Lainey softened her gaze, and spoke gently.

"You may not have said anything to make me feel guilty, Eve, but the way you would look at me told me how you really felt."

Eve recoiled as though Lainey had slapped her. She shook her head slightly, losing the fight she had in her. She thought she had successfully hid the pain she felt knowing Lainey and Jack were finding their way back to each other. Obviously she was wrong.

"You want it this way, Lainey, so be it. We'll do it your way."

She turned away, putting the SUV into gear and pulling back onto the road. She said nothing else to Lainey as they drove into the city to the gallery. It killed her that Lainey was doing this to her, but she wouldn't show it. This time she would be more successful at it. Eve Sumptor-Riley was well versed in hiding her feelings. She just never thought she would have to do it with Lainey after everything they've been through.

Eve's silence cut Lainey like a knife. She knew she was being unreasonable as Eve said, but Lainey couldn't help herself. She had been hurt when she and Jack showed up at Eve's house and Lainey saw plainly that Eve and Adam had been together. Yes, she knew she had no right to be upset. Yes, Eve had every right to be with her husband—without guilt—whenever she pleased. It was ridiculous for Lainey to behave the way she was. So, why couldn't she stop? Lainey needed to figure that out and quell it immediately before she lost Eve altogether.

Eve turned into the gallery's garage and smiled at Pauly.

"Good morning, Pauly." She was thankful that her voice was lighter than she felt.

"Good mornin', Mrs. Riley." Pauly stopped sucking in his gut and puffing his chest out whenever Eve came in. His priorities changed drastically two years ago. Besides, Eve was married now, off the market. Not that he had a chance in hell before—besides he was married, too—but, he saw it as an act of respect for Adam. The luckiest man on this green earth as Pauly saw it.

Eve shut it down again, giving Lainey nothing. Not even a glance as she pulled into the parking space and cut the engine. Opening the back door, she started unbuckling Bella, smiling warmly at her and cooing.

"Come on, baby girl. Momma has you."

Lainey's heart clenched at seeing Eve interact with Bella. She was such a natural mother. Lainey could remember the terror in Eve's eyes when Eve found out she was pregnant with Bella.

"*I lost my mother at an early age, Lainey. How am I going to do this? What if I fail?*"

Lainey reminded Eve of everything she's overcome, and though she did lose her mother at age fourteen, what her mother taught her up until then—not to mention the journal she left Eve—was more than enough to help Eve be a great mother. Lainey was right. Eve doted on Bella, but did it in a way that didn't spoil her. Too much.

"Let me help you." Lainey reached for Bella's diaper bag, but Eve hefted it onto her shoulder.

"I have it."

"Eve, please."

"I don't want to talk."

"Eve."

"*I don't want to talk, Lainey.*"

Eve's tone had Lainey's mouth snapping shut. Shit. She was going to have to do some serious begging to get out of the hole she just dug herself in. She stole a couple of glances at Eve on the elevator ride up to the gallery. Besides a scattering of grins to a murmuring Bella, Eve's face was set in a frown. When the doors opened to the gallery floor, Eve's face changed completely, taking Lainey by surprise. The look was pure pain and confusion.

"*Oh my God.*" Eve's voice was barely above a whisper, and Lainey barely registered the words before she turned to see what Eve saw.

Eve heard Lainey's gasp, but her focus was on the vision before her. The gallery—*her* gallery—was all but destroyed. Paintings and sculptures were scattered over the vast space, broken or damaged. Spray paint littered the wall that separated the space into a U shape in the middle of the room. Light fixtures were pulled from the ceiling, dangling menacingly above them. It was a disaster.

Eve stood frozen, her face a picture of torment. Seeing Eve like that grabbed Lainey's heart in an iron fist, squeezing painfully. Lainey had to reach out to stop the elevator doors from closing on them when Mikey came racing up to them.

"Mrs. Riley!"

Eve snapped out of her stupor, effectively hiding her emotions in a blink of an eye.

"Are you okay?"

Mikey blinked, surprised by Eve's question. Her gallery was ruined, but her first thoughts were of his safety. "Yes! I just got here a few minutes before you."

Mikey's eyes were rimmed red, and Eve knew he had been crying. Not because he was responsible, but because, Eve knew, he loved the art here almost as much as Eve herself. This was devastating for him. Not nearly as devastating as it was to Eve, but close.

"I called the cops," he continued. "I didn't touch anything! Oh …" He turned to look at the chaos again. "I can't believe this. Who would do this?"

It was a question Eve wanted the answer to, and fast. She lost everything once before. She'd be damned if she would go through that again.

"You and Lainey take inventory before the police get here. I want to know what is damaged and if anything is missing."

Mikey nodded solemnly while Lainey noted that Eve didn't look at her once when she spoke, not even when addressing her.

"I'm taking Bella up to the nursery, then I'll be in my office. Send whoever is in charge up when they get here."

"Yes, ma'am."

Mikey rushed away, and Eve started towards the stairs. She paused when she felt Lainey's hand on her arm.

"Eve."

Eve spared Lainey a glance, but was too raw to risk having Lainey say anything kind to her right now.

"Do your job, Lainey."

With Bella tucked safely away in the nursery, and Mikey and Lainey doing inventory, Eve retreated to her office. She had to pull in several deep breaths before calming herself enough to just think. Now, she stood at her huge, arched window and blindly watched the people below her. She had to remind herself over and over again that Tony was dead. There was no way he could be doing this to her. So, who was?

"Eve?"

Eve flinched at the intrusion of her thoughts, and confusion once again settled over her face. She turned, facing the man behind her.

"Captain Harris?"

His sandy blonde hair and full beard held a sprinkling of gray now. His golden brown, compassionate eyes had a few more wrinkles around them. Eve also noted the faint circles under them. He was tired, she thought.

Understandable. Two years ago, when he found out his partner was a murderer, and framing Eve, he had no choice but to go after him. When Maurice showed up at Eve's apartment to finish what her father, Tony, couldn't do, Harris—a detective then—had no choice but to use deadly force to prevent this.

Detective Charlie Harris was rewarded for his part in taking down Tony's operation, even being offered the job as Captain. Eve learned later that the captain preceding Harris was also on Tony's payroll.

Eve continues to think all of this was well deserved, but she could see now that what he had to do to his partner still weighed heavily on him. She went to him, kissed him lightly on the cheek, and offered him a small smile.

"What are you doing here, Charlie?"

"Investigating a crime."

Eve's brows furrowed deeper. "You're a captain now. And, this isn't a homicide. It's vandalism."

"It's you," he said simply, holding her gaze.

Eve's features softened, and she gestured to the chair in front of her desk. When she was settled in her own chair, she got down to business.

"Lainey and Mikey are taking inventory. I'll have a list for you as soon as they're done."

"And, after you've done the inspection yourself."

"They're more than capable."

"It's your gallery, Eve. You won't leave it to anyone else's hands, no matter how capable those hands are."

She stared at him for a moment. He was right. It unnerved her, just a little, that he saw that in her.

"You'll have the list soon," she said again.

"Good. Do you have any ideas on who would do this to you?"

Eve knew he was thinking about Tony.

"My father is dead, Charlie. You know I killed him. This can't be about him."

"Are you sure? Maybe associates, or someone he owed money to?"

"After two years? Why wait that long for a payout?"

"To catch you off guard."

His answer sent chills down Eve's spine. She shook it off, refusing to believe that this was about Tony. That part of her life was over. She made sure of that when she put two bullets into him, and taking one herself.

Harris saw the refusal in her eyes and changed directions.

"Do you have any enemies you can think of that would want to hurt you this way?"

Eve smiled grimly.

"I'm a successful woman, Charlie. You don't get that way without stepping on a few toes." She leaned back in her chair, lacing her fingers together. "It could be other gallery owners who don't like the fact that I can afford all of the priceless art. Or, protestors that think the art I feature is morally reprehensible. I have a drawer full of threats."

"Why have you never reported those threats?"

Eve laughed.

"I have been doing this a while, Charlie. If I were to report every threat I had from bible thumpers, I'd be known as the woman who cried wolf. You'd never know when the threat was actually real."

"It's real now."

"Yes, it is," Eve's mood turned somber.

Harris leaned forward, recognizing the resolve in Eve's eyes.

"Let me take care of this, Eve."

She held his gaze for a moment. "Billy can help."

Billy Donovan was an agent for the FBI, and though he helped Eve when she needed it with Tony, Harris didn't trust his motives.

"I don't think that's a good idea."

"Why?"

"I've seen the way he looks at you, Eve."

"You think he is attracted to me."

It wasn't a question, but a teasing statement. Still, Harris answered.

"He's a man. Of course he's attracted to you."

"You're a man, Charlie."

Harris shifted in his chair, uncomfortably. He couldn't deny feeling a certain attraction to Eve. Hell, he was a red-blooded male, wasn't he? But, he knew his boundaries. Harris wasn't so sure Agent Donovan did.

"I'm married."

"So is Billy. So am I." Eve sighed. She had to think about the gallery, not the feelings that people may or may not have for her. "He has connections beyond your jurisdiction, Charlie. Use his resources."

Harris nodded curtly. If this is what Eve wanted, he would give that to her.

"No one else, Eve. Let's keep this legal."

She knew he meant James. James often fell on the wrong side of the law. An occupational hazard, but extremely beneficial for anyone who needed answers.

"When this happened before it was just me, Charlie," Eve began. "I lost everything in the fire that destroyed my gallery before, but I survived and I rebuilt. Now, there are people here that I love."

She leaned in, pointing towards the furthest wall.

"My daughter is in the next room." Eve moved her point towards her door. "Lainey and Mikey are downstairs sorting through this mess. It's not just me anymore. I will do whatever I have to do to keep them safe."

Harris knew she meant that. She took a bullet, could have died, to save Lainey when Tony came to Eve's gallery that fateful night. Both women reported that Tony had surprised them, holding Lainey at gunpoint before Eve somehow talked him into letting her go. He couldn't know that Eve promised her father her body in exchange for Lainey's life. The report claimed that Eve and Tony struggled before the gun was discharged three times, hitting Eve once in the stomach and Tony twice, killing him.

"The last time you involved others, they got hurt or dead, Eve," he reminded her.

She raised an eyebrow in surprise. "I didn't involve Pauly, yet he was beaten—almost paralyzed—just so Tony could position a man in my parking garage. The only involvement Christine had in this was knowing where I went on vacation. She was severely beaten for information, which she lied about to protect me. Katherine involved herself with Tony. The only reason she is alive today is because I helped her. Meredith dug herself in too deep with dear old dad, not my doing. And, Jackie ..." Eve's voice wavered. She would feel guilty about Jackie until the day she died. The young woman had no involvement whatsoever in the battle between Eve and her father. Yet, she was murdered for the contemptible fact that Eve had spoken to her. While she may not have involved them herself, she knew all that happened was on her. She would cross lines if it kept everyone safe.

Eve sucked in a breath, releasing it slowly through her nose. "My resources go far beyond yours or Billy's," she continued. "Beyond the limits of the law. If that's what I have to do, that's what I will do ..."

"Stop talking, Eve." Harris lifted a hand. "I looked the other way two years ago. I'm a captain now. I can't look any way but the right way."

He stood.

"You do what you have to do. Just don't tell me about it."

Moving to the door, he paused and turned to Eve.

"Get me the list, and Agent Donovan's number. I'll have the best I have working on this. We'll be out of your hair as soon as we can."

Chapter Four

After Charlie left Eve, she emailed him Billy's information, emailed Billy with a head's up and emailed James with the new development. Eve knew she was taking the easy way out, not picking up the phone and discussing this personally, she just didn't care. Between Lainey and this mess, Eve was wiped. Completely, emotionally dispirited.

Eve bit back her sigh when she heard Lainey's light tap on her door. She couldn't even drum up the energy to call out.

Lainey waited, disheartened when Eve didn't respond. With a deep breath, she squared her shoulders and pushed the door open.

"Eve?"

"I can't, Lainey." Eve spoke quietly, her head shaking back and forth slowly. "I can't. I can't do this with you. Not now. I can't fight with you."

The despondency echoing through Eve's voice pained Lainey. Eve was strong, rarely showing emotion other than passion. For years, Eve didn't cry. Not even after her mother's death. Eve told Lainey that she was just unable to cry. It wasn't until Eve had deliberately hurt Lainey, in an effort to keep her safe, and Adam (for the same reason), that the tears came.

After that, Eve had been more forthcoming with her emotions, but only to a certain degree. She still kept her deepest feelings in check when she felt scrutinized.

"Eve, honey, I didn't come in here to fight with you. I came to apologize."

Eve stared warily at Lainey, saying nothing as Lainey planted herself in the plush leather chair in front of Eve's desk.

"You don't believe me."

Eve sighed. "Are you doing this because of what happened here at the gallery?"

"No." Lainey's body was stiff with fear, but she forced herself to relax. With a façade of calm, she sat back and crossed her legs. "I'm apologizing because I've been an idiot."

Eve could sense Lainey's internal struggle to remain casual. She rose slowly, striding over to sit next to Lainey. Her black pencil skirt and white button down shirt (with the top three buttons undone, of course), hugged her curves impeccably. Her red stilettos were high enough that when she sat and crossed her legs, the skirt inched up, and Lainey couldn't help but glance at the muscles that twitched in Eve's amazing legs.

Eve caught Lainey's glance, as well as the hungry look in her eyes before she wiped her expression clean. She felt the pang of desire and guilt hit her at the same time. Shit.

"Lainey, it's not idiocy. Do you think I don't feel what you feel? That I don't think about you, about what we had?"

"You don't show it," Lainey whispered.

"Because I know it would hurt you. I was selfish two years ago. No," Eve continued before Lainey could speak. "I was. I knew what you were going through with Jack, but I didn't stop what was happening between us."

"I didn't let you."

A small smile touched Eve's lips. "I was drowning, Lainey. I couldn't give myself to Adam. Not fully, and it killed me. He was slipping through my fingers and there was nothing I could do about it because I couldn't open myself up to him. You walked into my life, and I felt a breath. For once in all of those years since my mother died, I felt a breath."

Lainey's heart stuttered at Eve's admission. But she didn't have time to revel in it before Eve continued.

"When I met you, I felt a connection with you. I didn't know why at the time. In fact, I didn't realize the reason until much later." The wariness returned to Eve's eyes. She hoped what she had to say wouldn't hurt Lainey. "What we had, Lainey, was incredible. And, I was able to give you my heart because you were ... safe for me."

Lainey gasped softly. "That wasn't the only reason," she whispered. She remembered the first time Eve had told her she was safe. Lainey knew then, just as she knew now that it couldn't have been the only explanation of what happened between them.

"No. Of course it wasn't," Eve said quickly. "But, it's a big reason." Eve took Lainey's hand in hers, and continued. "You made it easy for me. You understood me, believed in me when I didn't believe in myself. You even encouraged me to be open with Adam."

"I could see how you felt about him. And, anyone with eyes could see he was in love with you."

Eve shook her head and chuckled. "You still say that even when talking about us." She rubbed her thumb across Lainey's knuckles. "My point is, Lainey, we were safe for each other. We gave each other something that each of us needed. But, when it came down to it, we made the choices we knew in our hearts were right."

"What if we made the choice out of fear?"

"Lainey, are you and Jack having problems?"

"No, I told you we're good. Which makes me feel horrible."

"You still love him."

"Of course I do."

"And, the sex?"

Lainey flushed slightly. "It's good. Better." She hesitated for a moment. "Better than it's ever been, actually."

Eve grinned. "That's good."

"It's great. I'm just confused."

"You saw Adam and me together, and you remembered what it was like for us. That's understandable. But, Lainey, you don't want to do that to Jack again. You don't want to be with me."

"I'm not so sure that's true, Eve."

Eve closed the distance between them, her lips a breath away from Lainey's, her palm resting on Lainey's cheek, and poised to kiss her. "Really?"

"*Eve.*" Lainey put her hands on Eve's shoulders. She didn't push, but she held her steady.

Eve smiled, shifted until her mouth was at Lainey's ear. "*That's what I thought.*"

Lainey sat back with a frustrated sigh. "I hate it when you do that. When you say something, or do something you don't mean just to prove a point." She explained when Eve looked at her questioningly. "You did it when you asked me to leave Jack and be with you and now this."

"I told you then that just because I knew what your answer was, that didn't mean I didn't mean it. Or don't want it."

"Ugh, you're just confusing me more."

"You're right, I'm sorry." Eve sat back, and clasped her hands in her lap. "My method is terrible, but it gets the message across."

"I agree on the method," Lainey mumbled. She was done with this conversation. If she wanted to get over these feelings (and she desperately wanted to), she needed to get her mind off of it. "I saw Captain Harris earlier."

"Yes." Eve obliged Lainey, and let the subject of the two of them go for now.

"Why was he here? There wasn't a murder." Lainey's eyes widened. "Was there?"

"No. He heard the call come in about the gallery, so he stopped in to see what he could do to help. He's going to work with Billy, and I have James on it as well."

Lainey blew out a breath. "Do they think this has something to do with Tony?"

"That's what everyone's first thought is."

"But, not yours?"

Eve sighed, and rubbed her temples to relieve the ache. "I don't know, Lainey. Maybe I'm being naïve, but I just can't see this being about Tony."

"What does Adam say?" Lainey watched Eve's eyelids lower. "You haven't told him?"

"We're not sure what this is. What's the point of worrying him over some vandalism?"

"He's not going to like that, Eve."

"He'll understand. Adam has so much going on, Lainey, I just want to have some idea of what's happening here before going to him." Eve stood and held her hand out to Lainey. "Until then, let's see what we can do about putting this place back together."

∝

Once the police were finished documenting, fingerprinting and basically making more of a mess in the gallery, Eve and Lainey got busy cleaning. Eve concluded that it was easier to have painters come in and repaint the walls, so they focused on the art. It hurt Eve's heart having to discard of such beautiful pieces. She knew that insurance would cover their costs, but money was never Eve's concern. Art has always been Eve's way to express herself, or to escape from the hell her life had been.

They separated what couldn't be salvaged from what Eve hoped she could restore. If it was too badly damaged for her, she would spare no expense in finding the best restorers in the country.

"Eve?"

"Yes, Mikey?"

"Ms. Cummings is here to see you."

Damn. Eve didn't need Dee Cummings, resident ace reporter, coming in to the gallery and asking God knows what. But, Eve didn't think she could turn her away. She had been instrumental in helping Eve bring down Tony and Maurice, even at the risk of her own life.

With an inward sigh, Eve stood and turned to face Dee. Always dressed to impress, Dee complimented her light coffee colored skin with apricot slacks and matching jacket. Her hair was swept up in a simple, modern chignon hairstyle that accentuated her high cheekbones, and left her piercing hazel eyes unobstructed.

"Dee. It's always nice to see you."

Dee laughed. "Right. I think the only time you thought it was nice to see me was at your wedding. And, that's because I bought you very nice China dinnerware. Hello, Lainey."

"Not true," Eve smiled, and instinctively took a protective step in front of Lainey. No matter what was happening between them, Eve would always want to shield Lainey from anything upsetting. "Though, it is a nice set. What can I do for you?"

"You could give me a statement about the break-in here."

Well, let's not beat around the bush, Eve thought. "I have no information. This just happened, Dee. The investigation has just begun. How did you hear about it, anyway?"

"I have my resources." Dee was cryptic as always, but Eve would get answers if she needed them. "Since it's so new, we'll just go through the basics. How do you feel? Do you have any ideas on who would do this?" She studied Eve. "Do you think this has anything to do with Tony?"

"Numb, no and no. There's my statement."

"Eve, I know Tony is dead, but …"

"But, nothing. Tony is dead and that's it. There's no more there. That part of my life is dead." Eve felt Lainey stiffen behind her. She hadn't meant the part with Lainey, but she couldn't very well say that now. Eve adjusted her stance insignificantly enough where Dee wouldn't notice, but Lainey would.

Eve's answers certainly didn't satisfy Dee, yet, she hoped it bought her some time. She took it as a positive sign when Dee dropped the subject. Eve knew, however, that Dee would be back, and she would be relentless. To her credit, Dee did promise to have her contacts look into things, and even though Eve knew this was more for Dee's benefit than Eve's, she didn't mind if it helped speed along the investigation.

For now, Eve was just ready to get home and put this day behind her. She didn't want to think about all of the memories this has drummed up. It hurt too damned much.

Chapter Five

The aroma of Eve's special spaghetti sauce filled the kitchen, along with the cooing and occasional word—or Bella's version of a word—from Eve's baby girl.

Eve glanced over at Bella, making a silly face, causing Bella to giggle. It was one of the most precious sounds to Eve, so she made it happen as often as she could.

Adam stood at the doorway of the kitchen and watched the two loves of his life. He couldn't stop the goofy grin he knew he had, but who could blame him.

"Are you just going to stand there, or are you going to come over here and kiss me?"

Adam's smile broadened. He loved how she could feel him when he was near. He walked up to her, wrapping his arms around her waist.

"Kiss you, of course," he whispered in her ear, and turned her to face him. His lips touched hers gently at first, until he felt her tongue touch his bottom lip. He deepened the kiss, their tongues tangling together, and when she fisted her hands in his hair, he pulled her closer against his hard body.

"Dada!"

Eve laughed softly against Adam's lips.

"Apparently your daughter wants some attention."

Adam groaned half-heartedly.

"We'll finish this later," he whispered, then turned and picked Bella up out of her highchair. "Hi there, little one. How's daddy's princess?"

Eve watched the two of them together, and her heart filled with such joy. Her family, she thought. She smiled at Adam when his eyes found hers. When she felt tears—happy tears—she turned back to the stove.

Adam watched Eve a little longer. So much had changed with her when it came to emotions. When they had first met, she made it clear to him that she wasn't looking for an emotional relationship. Of course, he fell in love with her the moment he met her. It killed him when she held him at arm's length for so long, but that was in the past. Eve had finally let him in, and it was even better than he had dreamt. Sleeping with her, waking up with her, being able to make love to her whenever he desired. And, boy did he desire her. All the time.

"I can hear your thoughts, baby."

"Can you? What am I thinking?"

"We'll discuss it later tonight. When we're alone." Eve glanced at Adam over her shoulder and winked.

"Works for me," Adam murmured. Bella patted Adam's cheek, and he knew what that meant. "Want a ride, do you?"

"Don't go too far, *amant*. Dinner is almost ready."

"We're not going too far, mommy. Just a short trip around the living room." Adam began making airplane sounds, and started 'flying' Bella around making her laugh.

Again, Eve's heart soared.

"Enjoy it while it lasts, Eve."

He watched her through binoculars. Disgust and anger filled him as he saw the happiness inside the beautiful home. It angered him that she had everything her heart desired, while he had nothing. The resentment almost took him over, and he wanted to end her now, but he fought it. She would know, first, what it was like to lose everything like he did. *She* took everything from him. It was her fault. He wouldn't stop until she has paid for what she's done.

"I have some news."

They were sitting at the dinner table, enjoying Eve's world class spaghetti—at least to Adam it was world class. Of course, he cherished every meal she made for him.

"Oh?" Eve's mind had been wandering, thinking about the gallery and the paintings she lost. She knew she needed to tell Adam, but what she said to Lainey was true. She didn't know exactly what was going on, so she would wait until she had information from Harris. She just hoped Adam would understand.

"I was asked to be a partner at the firm."

"Baby! That's wonderful!" Eve reached across the table to take Adam's hand. "I'm so proud of you. You deserve this so much."

The news solidified Eve's resolve to wait to tell Adam what was going on at the gallery. He did deserve this. And, he deserved to have his accomplishments celebrated without her ruining it with her problems.

"I'm not sure if I'm going to accept." Adam was hesitant. Eve was so excited about his being offered partnership, he wondered if she would be as excited by what he really wanted.

"Why wouldn't you accept?"

"I ..."

Eve saw his hesitancy, and left her own chair to sit on his lap.

"*Amant?* Are you afraid to tell me something?" Yes, Eve saw the irony in her question. Wasn't she not telling Adam everything?

"Not afraid, just not sure what you'll think." He wrapped his arms around her, loving the feel of her body close to his.

"I support your decisions no matter what they are. You know that."

Adam held her gaze, and saw she meant every word. "I was thinking of starting my own firm. Griffen Enterprises has agreed to come with me if I decide to leave. As have others I've brought in."

"They didn't sign exclusivity contracts?"

Always the astute business woman, he thought lovingly.

"Each of them signed a contract, yes, but reserve the right to change firms if they're not satisfied. My designs belong to the firm, but if I make slight changes that the client approves of, I think I can make it work."

"You've thought a lot about this."

"I wanted to tell you, beautiful." His arms tightened around her waist. "Please don't be upset. I just wanted make sure it's what I wanted first. When I was asked to be a partner today, I knew this was right for me."

Eve smiled and held his face in her hands. "I'm not upset, Adam. Of course, I wish you had talked to me, but I understand you needed to work this out for yourself."

"I'm asking you now, Eve. Do you think this is a good idea?"

"I think if this makes you happy, you should pursue it. I'm behind you one hundred percent."

"Yeah?"

Eve bent her head and kissed him. "Yeah," she whispered. "I love you, and I believe in you. Go for it, my love."

His hand snaked up her back and around the back of her neck. He flexed, massaging her while at the same time bringing her mouth back to his.

Before their lips could touch, a tiny hand full of spaghetti came flying through the air, landing partly on Adam's face and partly on Eve's.

Adam chuckled, swiping a finger down Eve's cheek. The sparkle in her eye told him she didn't mind the interruption one bit. In fact, she looked positively happy about it. Bella did that for her. She made Eve happy. And, Adam knew he did, too.

"Well, your little princess has made it clear she does not want to watch us make out."

The laughter in her voice overjoyed Adam.

"We'll just have to wait until later, I guess." He tugged Eve's arm when she moved to stand up. "Just know, when I get you alone I'm doing whatever I want to you."

"Mmm, I'm all yours, *amant*."

"Hello?"

"Hi, honey."

As always, the sound of Eve's voice made Lainey's pulse quicken.

"Is everything alright?"

"Yes, of course."

"Are you calling to check up on me? Afraid I'm still pining away for you?"

Eve let out a burst of surprised laughter. That deep, throaty, sexy laughter that Lainey loved so much.

"I'm going to venture a guess and say Jack isn't near."

"He's putting the boys to bed. Adam?"

"Putting Bella to bed," Eve answered. "And, no, I'm not checking up on you. I called to tell you that I'm having the nanny come and stay with Bella here at the house tomorrow. You and I are going to Branson's warehouse while the painters work on the gallery."

"Ugh, that man chaps my hide."

"Chaps your hide?"

"Stop laughing at me."

"How do you know I'm laughing?"

"I can hear it in your voice. Don't forget I know you."

"I could never forget that, Lainey."

Eve hadn't meant to flirt, or to drop her voice to a sultry whisper. Old habits, she thought.

Lainey cleared her throat. "Eve."

"Can you be here by eight?" she interrupted whatever else Lainey was about to say. Eve knew she probably shouldn't tease Lainey with the way she's feeling.

"Yes."

"Lainey, I never want to confuse you more or make you uncomfortable. Some things just …"

"Come naturally for you," Lainey finished. Eve was a flirter. She actually hopes Eve never changes that. Even if they can't be together, she finds it endearing that Eve would flirt with her. "Stop worrying. I'm sorting my feelings out. I want you to be you, and I like when you flirt with me. Don't let me ruin that by the way I've been acting lately."

There was a silence between them, but, oddly enough, it wasn't uncomfortable for the first time in the past couple of days.

"Hmm. I'll see you in the morning, honey." Eve watched as Adam strode in, stripping his shirt off in the process. "Get some rest." She waited for Lainey's goodbye and hung up the phone.

"Everything okay?"

"You're half naked. The only thing that could make it better is if you were fully naked."

Adam grinned. "Well, then. Who am I to disappoint my beautiful wife?"

Eve sat back against the headboard and watched as Adam unbuttoned his jeans, and slowly slid the zipper down.

"Are you enjoying this?"

"Immensely." Eve got to her knees on the bed, crooked her finger, beckoning him to come to her.

Adam climbed the platform, jeans undone, shirt off and completely aroused. He reached under the hem of Eve's t-shirt (his t-shirt that looked fucking amazing on her), bringing it up when his hands cupped her breasts.

"So beautiful."

Eve hooked her hands in his waistband, tugging his jeans down along with his boxer briefs.

"Now that's beautiful." Eve took Adam in her hand, stroking gently.

"He's very happy to see you."

Eve chuckled softly. "So I see. Now, do things to me."

"My pleasure."

He dipped his head and kissed her neck, trailing his tongue across her tanned shoulder. He moved lower, and she threaded her fingers through his hair, gasping when he pulls a nipple into his mouth. His tongue rolls in circles, making it hard and sensitive, while his hand caressed her other breast, pinching the nipple with just enough pressure to make her moan with pleasure. Adam gently pushed Eve down until she was laying on her back. Lifting her feet, he hooks her knees over his shoulders and bent his head to taste her.

Eve was desperate for him. Wet and anxious, she grasped at the back of Adam's head, pulling him closer to her. He rewards her by sweeping his tongue over her in a slow—and incredibly intense and pleasurable—rhythm.

"Baby, you're driving me crazy."

She felt his smile against her. He doesn't answer, just continues to torture her with sweet kisses, licking and sucking. She can feel herself getting close, and knows that he can feel it, too, because each time she's ready to go over, he changes the speed to bring her back down. Eve groaned in protest when his lips left her.

"Don't stop!"

She felt him shake with silent laughter, then he dipped his head again, and his tongue slipped inside her. The moan he emits when he feels her shudder because of his tongue vibrated through her, igniting more bliss.

"God that feels so good. Use your fingers, *amant*." She knows he loves to hear her tell him what she wants, and it's confirmed when she feels his hands flex on her hips before he gives in to her demands. One finger slides in her, and it's almost enough to make her go over.

"More!"

Two of his fingers are now sliding in and out of her, and she feels her body tense.

"Fuck! I'm coming, baby!"

Adam increases the pressure of his tongue and fingers, and she clenches around him as the orgasm washes over her. He stands up, wraps his arms around her thighs, and yanks her to him.

"I need to be inside you."

He growls when Eve wraps her hand around his cock, sliding him up and down her wetness before guiding him to her opening.

"Fuck me, Adam. Please."

He thrusts inside her, reveling in the strangled panting that comes from Eve as he drives her fast and hard. She wraps her legs around him, bringing her hands to his ass and pulling him deeper.

His cock is buried inside her to the root, and she still wants more, so he thrusts harder making her cry out.

"So fucking amazing!" His voice is hoarse with need, and he grunts with each assault, trying to keep his control. He pulls out suddenly, and Eve almost screams her disapproval. Then, she feels herself being flipped to her stomach, her hips being jerked back until her ass is against Adam's hard body.

She clutched the sheets as he pounded into her so hard her feet actually lift off the floor. Eve knows Adam's body so well, she can always tell when he's about to come. His cock grew harder—which always amazed her—and his body, his muscles, became so taut, it was solid against her ass as she pushed back into him. His grip on her hips is almost bruising, and she fucking loved it. She loved it even more when he roared her name as his own orgasm rocks him. With Adam driving into her harder, the friction and exquisite feel of him spurting hotly inside her, sends Eve over the edge again. She comes, hard, her body contracting around him, milking every last drop out of him.

"Wow!" Adam bends over Eve, still inside her. He rests his cheek on her sweat sheened back, waiting until both of their breathing starts to return to normal before kissing her, and gently pulling out of her.

Eve felt the warmth of his body as he laid next to her. Thoroughly fucked, she could stay where she was and not get up—ever—and she would be okay with that.

"We should probably get into bed and get comfortable."

"I'm good right here." Eve's words were muffled from being face-planted into the sheets.

Adam laughed, smacking her ass and making her yelp.

"Come on, beautiful. I want to hold you."

"So demanding," she muttered, squinting up at him with one eye. How the hell did he have so much energy? The way he had just hammered her, he should be as relaxed—and exhausted—as she was.

"You love it when I'm demanding."

"Only when we're fucking. Not when you're trying to get me to move when I think it's physically impossible."

Adam's eyes twinkled with humor watching her. So damned beautiful and sexy. And his. With renewed vigor, he stood, flipped Eve over on to her back ... and had a mind to take her all over again.

"Don't even think about it, pal. This area," Eve waved her hands in a circular motion around her crotch, "is closed for the next few hours."

"Closed, huh?"

"That's what I said."

"Bet I could get it to open up for me."

Eve narrowed her gaze at him. "Try it and it'll stay closed for a week," she threatened.

Adam threw back his head and laughed, and—damn her body—Eve responded with a quiet moan. Who did she think she was kidding? She knew, just as well as he did, she could never stay away from him for that long.

"Shut up."

He smirked at her, still tempted to have another go. "It's your own fault, you know. You're just too damn sexy for your own good."

The shadow crossed Eve's face for a split second before it cleared.

"Baby ..."

"Don't. Please don't apologize, Adam."

"I should have chosen my words better, Eve."

This is what she didn't want, what she had always avoided by not revealing her past. Eve never wanted Adam, or Lainey, to think about what she had been through as a mere child. The unspeakable things she had to do with her body. Those men had paid for her because she was 'too beautiful' to resist. But, that was then. And, this was Adam. She wouldn't let her past hurt them anymore.

"I don't want you to have to worry about what you say to me."

"I made you think ..."

"No. Look, the words are something of a trigger. I can't help where my mind goes when I hear them. But, when I'm with you, when you're touching me, kissing me, making love to me, none of that other stuff ever happened. Do you understand?"

Adam sat down next to her, and cupped her cheek in his hand. "It did happen."

"Not when I'm with you." Her words were an urgent plea for him to comprehend. "Everything else goes away when you're near me. When you're inside me, it feels like I've never been touched by anyone but you. I want you to forget about it like you make me forget. Please."

Her words touched him deep in his soul. It never ceased to amaze him how strong Eve was. To go through being tortured the way she was, violated in the worst way a woman could be violated, and still be the generous, loving woman she was, astonished him.

Knowing that he made her forget that awful time in her life, humbled him.

He brought her lips to his, kissing her gently. Then smiled into her eyes. "Nothing outside of this house exists, beautiful. Just you, me and our baby girl. Let's go to sleep."

They snuggled together, her back to his front, and slept dreamlessly.

Chapter Six

"I'll get it, Lexie," Eve called when the doorbell rang. She peered in the kitchen as she passed by, and saw the nanny wiping oatmeal off of Bella's face. Eve smiled at the scene. Bella loved the young, fun-loving and sincere brunette—though that wasn't necessarily a difficult thing for Bella—and, Lexie was excellent with her. Eve couldn't be happier to have her there. She especially liked the fact that Lexie had multiple certifications in childhood education, and felt comfortable leaving Bella in Lexie's care.

Eve opened the door, and frowned. "Lainey? Since when do you ring the doorbell?"

"Good morning to you, too." Lainey pushed past Eve. "I rang the doorbell because I didn't want to interrupt anything."

Eve didn't detect any hostility in Lainey's voice, but she still didn't like it.

"Before you start bitching at me," Lainey smirked at Eve's raised brow. She knew not many people had the nerve to talk to Eve that way. "I'm just trying to be more respectful."

"Fuck respectful, Lainey." Eve's voice was low, and if Lainey admitted it, kind of scary. "You are welcome in this house, *without* having to ring the damn doorbell."

"Calm down. I thought perhaps you and Adam may still be celebrating, so I was just being careful."

Eve couldn't hold back the smile thinking of her night with Adam. She bumped Lainey's shoulder. "You do realize we have a daughter, and Lexie is here, right? What would we possibly be doing?"

Lainey caught Eve's smile, and even though she felt the slight sting of jealousy, she was happy for them.

"Actually, I forgot Lexie was going to be here."

"Oh? You must have had a good night, as well." The smile Eve gave Lainey was wicked, and knowing. Lainey flushed slightly, because Eve was very right. Her night with Jack had been better than good. In fact, it had been amazing. She felt Eve's hand take hers as Eve pulled her towards the kitchen. "Coffee?"

Lainey cleared her throat—and, her mind of the night before—and grinned. "Yes, please."

∞

"What will happen if they can't find the paintings?" Lainey sipped coffee from her to-go mug. They pulled into the parking lot of Branson's delivery warehouse, and Eve swung into a parking spot and cut the engine.

"Insurance will get involved, and we'll have a lengthy period in which they'll investigate, try to devalue the paintings and then bitch and moan while writing out the check."

Lainey's shoulders shook with silent laughter at Eve's answer. It was a terrible situation, but she was glad Eve could find a little bit of humor.

"You're hoping they find them." Of course she would rather have the paintings than the money. That was how Eve was. The money wasn't worth as much as the art to her. Lainey knew that art may have been the one thing that saved Eve's sanity, perhaps even her life, during that horrid time in her past.

"Hmm. I'm not getting my hopes up. Those paintings could be halfway around the world by now."

Or, somewhere too close to home, Lainey thought silently. She still wasn't convinced that this had nothing to do with Eve's father. She had no idea how or why, but she couldn't shake the feeling. It was ridiculous really. Tony was dead, and Eve didn't think it was related. She just wished she could trust Eve's instincts. Despite the warm spring air, Lainey shivered at the thought.

"Cold?" Eve was at Lainey's side then, and rubbed her hands down Lainey's arms a couple of times to warm her up.

"Not really. Someone walking over my grave, I guess." Lainey's mumbled reply was a bit distracted by the thoughts that came into her mind when Eve's hands were on her. She shut it down, quickly, and smiled. "Let's get this over with. The less time I have to spend near that man, the better."

Eve shook her head with a smile at Lainey's back. Lainey had once been very timid, thinking she was just a boring old mom. After their affair, Lainey's attitude changed completely. Even becoming quite bold, as Eve remembered affectionately. The new Lainey kept Eve on her toes every day. It was an adventure Eve enjoyed a lot.

"Ms ... er, Mrs. Riley! I told you I would contact you if I had any information!" Mr. Branson's chubby face reddened with frustration.

"I'm not very good at waiting, Mr. Branson. I would like to take a look around."

"Absolutely not! This is *not* a gallery."

"Clearly." Eve scoffed. Her surroundings were deplorable to say the least. Thinking of precious art in the dingy, stuffy warehouse made her shudder. She was seriously considering opening her own distribution center just to cut Branson out. It was certainly something to evaluate, she thought as she deliberately walked past Branson.

"You cannot go back there!" Branson positioned himself between Eve and the entrance to the expansive area holding paintings and sculptures encased in cloth or brown paper wrappings.

"Watch me."

"Mrs. Riley, don't you need a warrant or something to come crashing in here and searching my place of business?"

"She's not the law, Mr. Branson. No warrant is necessary." A man in a dark suit stepped inside, and stood in front of Branson.

He—seemingly appearing from thin air—startled Lainey who had been enjoying the showdown between Branson and Eve. She recognized his face, but couldn't place it with a name.

"Well, then I am forbidding her to inspect my place." Branson crossed his arms, defiantly, clearly thinking that was the end of the conversation.

Lainey snickered. The man obviously did not know Eve.

"Mr. Branson, you have lost millions of dollars of my client's merchandise."

Ah, so *that's* who he is. Eve's lawyer. Lainey still couldn't think of his name.

"I would say she has every right to be here and look around, don't you? Unless you'd rather make this a messy legal battle?"

Eve chuckled as Branson sputtered. "Don't you just love lawyers?" Once again, she walked past Branson, motioning for Lainey to follow her, and began rummaging.

"You asked your lawyer to be here?"

Eve flipped through paintings that were leaned, haphazardly, against the wall, and glanced at Lainey.

"When that amount of money is involved, lawyers usually are, too. But, to answer your question, no, I didn't ask Ian to be here. He insisted."

"What are we looking for?"

"Nothing." Eve grinned mischievously. "I just want to rattle Branson. And, see what I'm dealing with."

"Eve! You are so naughty!" As soon as the words left her mouth, Lainey knew it was the wrong choice. She saw Eve's eyes flash, and Lainey felt the heat build inside herself. Damn it.

"*It will always be there, Lainey.*" Eve whispered. "*It was too deep, too intense to just disappear.*" She touched a fingertip to Lainey's lips, before dropping her hand and going back to the paintings.

Lainey blew out her breath, fluffing out her bangs. She knew nothing would happen between her and Eve again. But, the hell if she wasn't going to fantasize—just a bit.

Eve saw more paintings through a door that was slightly ajar, so she pushed it open and went in. Ian was keeping Branson busy in the front office, so Eve was going to take liberties with her exploration.

"Should we be in here?"

Eve shrugged in answer to Lainey's question. She didn't care if she couldn't be in here. As far as she was concerned, Branson owed her. Eve was planning her takeover of Branson's delivery service when she saw them.

"Son of a bitch!"

"Eve?"

"That fucking asshole!"

"Eve! What is … oh my God! Is that …?"

"Mine? Yes."

"But, why would he tell you it was missing? And, where are the rest?"

"Let's go find out."

Eve's deliberate stride was full of rage—and, quite sexy if Lainey took time to think about it—as she made her way to Branson.

"What the fuck are you trying to pull, Mr. Branson?"

"Excuse me?"

He looked scared, and guilty as shit, Eve thought.

"Why do you have one of *my* paintings hidden away here?"

Ian instantly perked up.

"I have no idea what you're talking about!"

"Bullshit! Don't fucking lie to me!" Eve closed the distance between them, and lowered her voice. "You don't want to know what happened to the last person that lied to me."

She thought of Meredith. Of course, Eve didn't have anything to do with Meredith's death, but had she been honest with Eve and let Eve help her, Meredith would be alive today.

Lainey stepped up, and placed her hand on Eve's arm, pulling her back. She understood how upset Eve was, but she didn't want Eve to think about the terrible things that happened.

"Mr. Branson," Lainey said amicably, even though she did not have one amiable bone in her body for this so-called man. "Eve and I saw one of her paintings in an office back there."

"Do you always take it upon yourself to go into places you're not welcome?"

Lainey's hand tightened on Eve's arm when she, again, stepped toward Branson.

Ian advanced then, taking Eve's place.

"I can have an investigator here within minutes, Mr. Branson. Not to mention the police. You may want to start explaining."

"She's mistaken." Branson tugged at his collar, and sweat gathered on his mustache.

"Eve does not make mistakes when it comes to art," Ian replied, coldly. "If she says it's hers, I believe her."

Branson's mouth clamped shut.

"Have it your way." Ian brought out his phone, ready to call the investigators.

"Call Captain Harris."

Eve's voice was eerily quiet, and her eyes never left Branson.

"You want to call the police in?" Ian was surprised. Eve usually preferred to take care of problems in her own way. A way that normally didn't require the law.

"No. I want Captain Harris here. Ask him not to say anything." She knew she had no right to ask Charlie to keep quiet, but Branson only had one of her paintings that she saw. If she wanted to find the rest, and get answers, she needed Branson to talk *without* lawyers. But, she also wanted to keep Charlie in the loop, just in case. "Call James, as well."

Ian's eyes widened a bit. A police captain, and a known criminal in the same place? Only Eve could pull that off without a hitch, he thought, and made the calls.

⚮

"Legally, I cannot conduct a search without Mr. Branson's permission or a warrant, Eve."

"I can." James began to move towards the office before Harris stopped him.

"If you want me to be able to do anything about this, it has to be by the book."

"I can get the painting, and make him talk," James sneered. Cops had too many damn rules!

"Enough." Eve stepped between Charlie and James. "I saw the painting, Charlie. So did Lainey."

Harris took Eve aside so Branson couldn't hear. "Eve, he could easily say you planted that painting there, and if he has a good lawyer, that's exactly what they'll tell him to say. Lainey is your assistant. She would lie for you."

Eve's eyes cut to Charlie. "You know, as well as I do, that Lainey would not lie about this."

"You're right. *I* do know. But, do you think anyone else would see it that way?"

When Eve frowned, Harris continued.

"Let me do this by the book, Eve."

He sighed when Eve slowly shook her head. "I need answers, Charlie. You mentioned his lawyer. If you arrest him, I can't get him to talk without an attorney present. Which means I don't get what I need. The painting is there. I just need to know why, and where the others are. James can get answers."

"Eve! Damn it!" Harris watched Eve retreat back to James, and speak softly to him. With another sigh, he took out his phone and made a call.

Eve's phone rang, and she saw Billy's name pop up on the ID. Once again, her eyes went to Charlie. He had called him, she was sure, she just didn't know what he thought that would accomplish.

"Billy."

"Eve, what you're doing is illegal."

"He has my painting. What I'm doing is finding out what happened to the rest of my belongings."

"Then let Harris do it."

"Did he really think you could talk me into this?"

She heard Billy's exasperated breath, and almost smiled. If she weren't so damned pissed, she probably would have.

"No. I think he's smarter than that," Billy muttered. "Hand the phone to Branson. Harris thinks hearing from the FBI can intimidate him enough to talk before we have to arrest him."

"It's for you." Eve handed the phone to Branson, then joined Charlie. "You're so hung up on going by the book. Tell me, Charlie. What would you arrest him for? You said yourself you can't search this place without a warrant. I doubt you could arrest him for being an asshole."

Charlie didn't even bother trying to hide his smile. "Could you imagine how full the jails would be if we arrested people for being assholes? I would ask him to come to the station to answer questions, as a person of interest in the case of the Sumptor Gallery thefts."

"And, if he refused?"

"Then, I'd arrest him for being an asshole. Or, obstruction of justice."

Eve laughed, softly, but sobered quickly when she saw defiance in Branson's face as he spoke to Billy. "He won't tell you anything."

"So, I should let James beat it out of him?"

Eve entertained the thought for a moment. She didn't care for violence, having seen too much of it in her life. But, she also didn't care for being stolen from.

"He wouldn't beat him. Just intimidate him. More so than what Billy is doing, it seems."

Eve had had enough. She strode over to Branson, and snatched the phone from his hand.

"This isn't working, Billy. I'll call later." She disconnected, glanced at James—who walked up behind Branson—then brought her eyes back to Branson. "I'm finished playing games with you. Why do you have my painting?"

"Go to hell. I don't have to talk to you."

James grabbed Branson around the back of the neck, and leaned in. "The lady asked you a question." He squeezed. "Answer her."

"Are you going to allow this?" Branson fumed at Harris.

Captain Charlie Harris turned and walked out of the building.

"Where are you going?!"

James changed his stance, clutching Branson around the throat and slamming him against the wall. "I said answer her!"

"Eve?" Lainey's timid touch quivered on Eve's shoulder.

"It's okay, Lainey. Why don't you keep Charlie company outside?"

"I want to stay with you."

Eve turned to her and smiled. "I'd rather you go outside. Everything will be fine. I'll join you in a minute."

Lainey saw the determination in Eve's eyes, and reluctantly agreed. "*Please hurry,*" she whispered, then disappeared outside.

Eve nodded to Ian, then waited until he was gone before stepping closer to Branson.

"Don't *fuck* with me. Why do you have my painting?"

James dug his fingers into Branson's neck at his continued silence, only backing off when Branson turned red, and started coughing.

"It was payment!"

"Payment for what?"

"They will kill me if I talk!"

"Who says *I* won't kill you if you don't," James growled.

"James."

James grudgingly backed off at Eve's urging.

"Who will kill you, Branson?" Eve exhaled with frustration when Branson said nothing. "I can't help you if you don't talk to me."

"Is she still in there with him?"

"Yes, sir. She's trying to get him to talk." He spoke through the headset, watching Eve through the scope of his rifle, then focused back on Branson. "What would you like me to do?"

"Take him out before he says anything."

"What about Eve?"

"Not yet." Damn, it would be so easy to kill Eve now and be done with this. But, he would wait and watch her suffer first. "Where is the other woman?" Perhaps if Eve watched her friend die, that would be the beginning to Eve's end.

"Outside, with the cop."

Fuck. It was unfortunate that the woman was not next to Eve. Luck won't always be on your side, bitch, he thought.

"Deal with Branson. Perhaps scare them a little, but no other casualties. Yet. We'll leave them for later."

The call was disconnected. He had a job to do. He aimed, and pulled the trigger.

∞

"Branson ..." Eve felt the warm splatter of blood hit her face, and stood there, confused as she watched Branson's body slump to the floor.

"What the fuck just happened?" She felt James push her out from in front of the window, and cover her body with his. Concrete ricocheted from the walls as more shots came through.

"Eve!" Lainey came running through the door at the commotion, but couldn't see Eve. Only James, and a very dead Branson.

"Get her out of here, Harris!" James yelled his order through gritted teeth.

"Lainey, let's go!" Harris radioed in to dispatch as he ran behind Lainey, shielding her from the direction of the shots. "Shots fired! Shots fired! 5153 is on scene. Get units here, now!"

"Charlie! Eve is in there!" Lainey felt the hot trail of tears flow down her cheek. Was Eve hit? Was she alive? If she was shot, how was she going to go through this again?

"James is with her! Get down! I need to make sure you're safe before I can go back in."

It seemed like a goddamn eternity before Eve was able to leave the building and see for herself that Lainey was unharmed. Police officers flooded the building, and Eve was questioned before being released.

When she stepped outside, she saw Lainey and immediately went to her, wrapping her arms around her. Eve held Lainey closer, feeling Lainey's body shake with sobs.

"It's okay. I'm fine. Shh, baby, I'm fine. I'm right here."

"You have blood on you."

"It's Branson's, honey. Not mine."

"What happened? God, Eve, I was so scared!"

"I know. Me too. I have no idea what happened. One minute, we were talking to him, the next his brains were scattered on the wall."

Eve cursed softly when Lainey's body jolted.

"I'm sorry, Lainey. I shouldn't have said that."

"Eve?"

She turned to look into Charlie's worried eyes.

"You should take Lainey home. I'll stay here and get as much information as I can." He paused for a moment, watching her. "This is now a murder investigation. My jurisdiction."

"It wasn't me, Charlie."

"I know. I was here, remember?"

"I mean, it wasn't me they were after. I was two feet away from Branson. If they wanted me dead, it would have been easy."

Lainey gasped, and clung to Eve's hand.

Harris nodded, but he wasn't sure Eve was entirely right. Multiple shots were fired. The shooter could have just missed his target. "I'll get info, and give you what I can. In the meantime, stay out of this. Let me handle it. This isn't just about stolen art anymore."

Chapter Seven

Eve dropped Lainey off before pulling into her own driveway next to Adam's car. He was home early, and she had blood splattered all over her. Perfect. She blew out a breath, and sat there for a minute, laying her head back on the headrest. She had hoped to be able to take a shower, and get her thoughts together before having this conversation with Adam. So much for that. And, after what happened today, there was no keeping it from him anymore. With a deep breath, she got out of the car and went inside to face her husband. Shit. He's going to be pissed.

Adam was furious. Eve had promised him she wouldn't keep things from him anymore, and he had to hear what was going on from Agent Fucking Donovan. It pissed him off even more that Donovan was in on this, since Donovan clearly had feelings for Adam's wife. He heard her pull into the driveway—this time his heart was pounding out of anger more than lust—and waited. She must know he wasn't happy, because she's taking her sweet damn time coming in the house. Adam took a deep breath to try and calm himself when he heard the door open. He would give her a chance to explain. At least, that was his plan before she walked in covered in blood.

"What the fuck, Eve?!"

"Where is Bella?"

"Jack and the boys are watching her. So, again, I ask; what the fuck?"

"Baby ..."

"Don't! You're covered in *fucking blood*!"

Oh yeah, he's pissed.

"It's not mine," she said evenly.

Adam threw his hands in the air. "Well, thank fuck for that!" His eyes bore into hers. "Why did you keep this from me?"

Eve's brows furrowed in confusion. How did he already know?

"I got a fucking call from Donovan, Eve."

Fuck. That, for sure, pissed him off more. She knew Adam didn't trust Billy's feelings for her.

"What did he say?"

"I want to hear what *you* have to say!"

"Baby, I'm covered in blood. I watched a man die today ..."

"It really sucks that that isn't the first time that's happened to you, Eve. What sucks even more is I am, *once again*, the last fucking one to know!" He roared.

Eve dropped to her knees and buried her face in her hands. Exhaustion, dread, regret—so many damned emotions hit her at once—she no longer had the strength to deal with it now. "*I'm sorry.*"

Adam expected excuses, a fight, even a defiant Eve. Not this broken woman before him. This wasn't how Eve was. She was strong, determined and confident. Flawed, yes. But, his perfection.

His anger was conquered by this weary Eve. He came to her, silently picking her up and carrying her to their bathroom upstairs. Adam gently sat her on the closed toilet seat and began undressing her.

"I liked that shirt," she said quietly when he threw her baby blue, silk shirt in the trash.

"I'll buy you a new one," he murmured, reaching to turn on the shower. "Up."

Eve stood, wondering how her legs were working when she was so bone tired.

Adam stripped her, throwing all of her clothes away. He was sure the blood would come out, but Eve wouldn't need reminders of this day. He took his own clothes off, then wrapped his arms around her.

"Hold on to me." Even her grip around his neck was weak, he thought, as he lifted her and walked her into enormous shower. Normally their shower was one of their favorite places to make love. With its light emperador marble and pulsating, ambient lighted shower heads that surrounded them from calf to head, it added another element of sensation for them. Tonight, though, Adam just hoped it washed away what was hurting Eve. He placed her on the bench that lined the wall, turned the shower heads towards her, and grabbed the sponge and body wash.

"Do you want to talk about it?"

It felt good having him wash her. She didn't want to talk or think, she just wanted to feel him. Eve shook her head when he reached up to wash her face free of blood.

He cupped her face in his hands when it was clean. "You have to tell me what's going on, beautiful. I can't be on the outside again. Do you understand?"

"Yes."

Her voice was so small, so quiet, so unlike Eve, it scared him. She's been through so much, he wondered if she had finally hit a point where she couldn't take anymore.

"Let's get you to bed."

He moved to get up, stopping when she held on to his hand.

"*Hold me.*"

Adam sat next to her, pulling her onto his lap. He cradled her there while she wept silently.

"I asked Lexie to watch Bella here at the house. Indefinitely." Adam set Eve's coffee cup in front of her. He made it extra strong today. She had tossed and turned most of the night, so he felt she could use the pick me up.

"You don't think she's safe with me."

It wasn't a question, but he answered anyway.

"I don't think *you're* safe, but I can't control what you do." Unfortunately, he added silently. "I can control what my daughter does."

"Your daughter?" Eve couldn't blame him for being worried, but damn, that hurt. She should actually be relieved. He was handling this a lot better than she thought.

"*Our* daughter," he amended. "I don't want her at the gallery until we know what's going on. And, I mean *we*, Eve. You need to start talking to me."

"Baby, I was going to tell you everything."

"When, Eve? After it's all over with and you finally let me out of a room you've lock me in?"

Eve flinched at the sarcasm and hurt in his voice. She should have been prepared for him to bring up that night Maurice was shot in her bedroom.

Eve had taken Adam to the secret studio she had had built in her apartment in the city when her neighbor, Mrs. Jenkins, warned her that Maurice was in the hall. She locked him in there to keep him safe, and Adam was livid when she finally opened the door. It took her months of apologizing—and, copious amounts of sexual acts—for him to forgive her. Even trying to explain to him that because she had just learned how to let him in her heart, the fear of losing him was too much for her, didn't work.

"It was forgeries and vandalism, Adam, not murder. At least not until yesterday. I wanted something solid to tell you before coming to you and ruining your week."

"Ruining my week?"

"You have been so happy, *amant*. You got this great account, was offered partnership, decided to venture out on your own. I didn't want to spoil that with my shit."

Adam stared silently at her for a moment before sighing.

"We're married, Eve. That means whatever we're going through, good or bad, we share it. For better or worse, remember? We don't keep things from each other. Especially things this important." He went to her and tilted her chin up to look at him.

"You could have died yesterday. I would have lost my wife, and Bella, her mother, and I wouldn't have had any clue as to why."

His voice was rough as he tried to swallow the lump that formed. Thinking about what could have happened scared the shit out of him.

"I'm sorry, baby." Eve reached up and kissed his mouth gently. "I honestly thought this was just some stupid incident from either my competition or some whacked out religious group. I didn't think it would come to this."

"Does this have to do with your father?"

Eve exhaled, harshly. "I don't know. If you had asked me before yesterday, I would have said no, it's impossible. But, now? I just don't know."

"Besides Donovan, who's on this?"

"Charlie. Especially after Branson's murder. And, James."

"You called James?"

Adam appreciated the fact that James helped Eve with Tony, but having a criminal involved wasn't ideal for Adam. Particularly when Bella was with Eve most of the time.

Eve rose a perfectly sculpted eyebrow. "I trust him, Adam," she said, reading his thoughts. "And, I thought he could find information if the paintings were being sold on the black market."

Their brief staring contest was interrupted by the chiming of Eve's phone.

"It's Lainey," she told Adam before answering. "Good morning. Did you sleep okay?" Eve sat heavily in the chair, fighting fatigue that wanted to swallow her up. She felt guilty for putting Lainey in the middle of a dangerous situation. Again. Jack was probably pissed at her. Which sucked, because Jack and Eve's relationship—for what it was—had began to be cordial after Eve took a bullet to save Lainey's life. Though Eve knew he would always blame her for Lainey's involvement in the first place. Even so, a mutual—silent—peace agreement was made for Lainey's sake.

"Good morning. Yes. You?"

"Mmhmm." Eve hadn't slept well, but she didn't need Lainey worrying about her.

Lainey hesitated, then drew in a shaky breath. "Eve, I told Jack everything that was going on."

"Good." She glanced at Adam who sat next to her, and was watching her intently. "He should know everything."

"Well, now that he does, he doesn't want me going in to the gallery. At least not until they find the shooter. I'm so sorry."

"Don't be. It's understandable." She was disappointed, of course. But, honestly, could she blame Jack for the request?

"Are you going?"

"I'm not sure, yet." Adam hadn't made the same request. Would he? And, would she comply?

"Did you talk to Adam?"

"Yes."

"Is everything okay?"

Eve paused as she looked at Adam. She saw in his eyes that he was hurt and angry, but he kept calm when talking to her. Calm before the storm? God, she hoped not.

"Yes. Honey, Lexie will be here in a little bit, and Adam and I need to finish talking. Can I call you later?"

"Of course! I hope you don't go to the gallery, Eve. If you do, please be careful. I'm going to worry about you."

Eve couldn't respond in the way she would like to Lainey, so she just said her goodbyes and hung up.

"Does Jack know?" Adam asked as Eve set her phone down.

"Yes."

"And? How does he feel about it?"

"He doesn't want Lainey going to the gallery until we know something."

"Is Lainey agreeing to that?"

"Yes." She saw the pain in his eyes, and knew he thought she wouldn't do that for him. For some reason, knowing he felt that way, saddened her. "Ask me."

Adam frowned. When the confusion lifted, he knew exactly what she meant.

"Will you stay home?" He took her hands in his. "Please? Stay home where I know you'll be safe?"

"I will."

Relief filled his face so quickly it almost knocked the breath out of her.

"Can I ask you something, Adam?" When he kissed her knuckles and nodded, she continued. "Are you going to start yelling at me, or punish me at some point? I'd rather know now instead of waiting for it."

To her surprise, Adam laughed. "Is that what you've been waiting for?"

"I have. I waited for it last night. Now, I'm sitting here, my coffee is getting cold, I need to go wake our daughter up and get her ready for Lexie, and all I can do is think about when you're going to react to all of this."

"This is my reaction, Eve."

"Adam, you made me *beg* for forgiveness the last time I kept something like this from you."

"Oh, I'll make you beg, again, and I'll definitely punish you. But, that will be when we have more time. As for now, this is my reaction."

Eve's pulse picked up quite considerably when Adam told her he'd make her beg. Seriously, Adam's "punishment" in bed was *almost* worth getting shot at. Still, he was just too damn calm for her to believe this was it.

Adam rose from his chair, bringing her with him, and wrapped his arms around her.

"I got the call, then I saw you with blood all over you, and I was pissed, Eve. So pissed I wanted to say things to hurt you as much as I was hurting. Then I saw that you were already hurting. Your life has been full of pain, beautiful. I don't want to be a part of that pain." He kissed her temple. "Just don't keep anything else from me, yeah?"

Eve took Adam's face in her hands, and brought his mouth to hers for a mind-blowing kiss. In that moment, with her kissing him like that, Adam could forgive Eve for anything.

Chapter Eight

"I'm glad you didn't go in to the gallery today, Eve." Lainey took party favors out of bags, and stacked them on the table.

"Adam asked me not to. After everything that's happened, I owed him at least that."

Lainey glanced over at Eve. Her mood had been off today, rightfully so, Lainey thought, but still not like Eve. Lainey wondered if Adam was more upset than Eve told her.

"Are you two doing okay?"

"We're fine."

"Eve, you know you can talk to me, right?" Lainey didn't want Eve to think just because Lainey was having these feelings, Eve couldn't come to her about Adam.

"I know." Eve stopped unpacking bags and sighed. "He was pissed at me. Seriously pissed, and I don't blame him. But, he stopped. Just stopped being pissed. I guess I'm waiting for the other shoe to drop."

"Did you ask him about it?"

"Yes. He told me that I had too much pain in my life, and he didn't want to be a part of that."

"That's sweet, Eve."

Eve made a sound, and went back to the bags. Bella's birthday party was two days away, and Eve was glad to have something to occupy her mind. She wasn't used to stepping back and letting others take care of things for her, but what more could she do for the gallery? It was still being cleaned up, the pieces evaluated or restored and Harris and James were working on the Branson connection. All Eve could do now, was wait. Not her best attribute.

"You don't think it's sweet?" As Eve thought about how she was going to steer clear of the gallery for however long, Lainey wondered about Eve's ambiguous murmur.

"I do."

"But?"

Eve blew out an exasperated breath, debating on how much she want to tell Lainey. Then she remembered that Lainey was the one other person she could be completely honest with, and know she will not judge. Eve peered out the kitchen door to make sure Lexie and Bella were not in ear shot. When she saw them engrossed in an educational game, she looked back at Lainey.

"I broke down, Lainey. I couldn't help it, could do nothing to stop it. I just fell to my knees in front of him and broke down. I can't help but wonder if that's why he stopped being pissed. Perhaps he thinks I'm losing it."

"Oh, honey." Lainey's heart broke a little hearing Eve talk about losing control. "He doesn't think you're losing it. Adam just understands you've been through more than your fair share of shit."

Eve couldn't help the burst of laughter. Lainey wasn't one to curse a lot (unless she was mad), so when she did, it tickled Eve.

"I know, I'm just not used to him seeing me like that."

"You're married, Eve. He sees you, and loves you, for better or worse."

Eve's eyes cut to Lainey, again. "That's basically what he said. You would think that almost two years in, I'd get that." She knew she should believe in that, but that person who broke down is not who Adam married. He married a strong woman. Not some weak, emotional woman. It just wasn't a pleasant feeling for Eve.

"You've held your emotions in for so long, Eve, that I'm sure it's going to take a while to feel comfortable letting them out."

Before Eve could respond, Bella tottered into the kitchen towards Eve, her arms lifted.

"Mama!"

Eve bent and scooped Bella up, wrapping her in her arms. "Hi, baby girl. Are you hungry?"

"Sorry, Mrs. Riley! I was putting up the game, and she just ran off! Fast little bugger!"

"Not a problem, Lexie. Have you had lunch?"

"No ma'am. I was going to wait until after I fed little Bella here."

"Would you like a sandwich?"

"Oh! Ma'am, I can make something! I don't want to take you away from anything."

"Don't be silly. I'm going to make something for Bella, Lainey and myself. I can certainly make you something. Do you like turkey?"

Lexie blushed shyly. None of the families she had ever worked for were interested enough in her to be more than cordial. She wasn't sure how to react to Eve's kindness.

"Yes, ma'am."

"Lexie? Please, call me Eve. I think you've worked for us long enough to be on a first name basis." Eve smiled warmly at her, and watched Lexie tentatively smile back. "Is turkey good for you, Lainey?"

Lainey grinned, and nodded. Eve's compassion never ceased to amaze her.

∞

After lunch, Eve put the finishing touches on the guest list for Bella's party. The list included Lainey's boys, the other young ones Lexie teaches, Henry, Trudy and Stevie, Mikey and his mother, Pauly and his family, Billy and his wife and kids—much to Adam's disappointment—Charlie and his wife, and, to make things even more interesting, James and his family. Eve's eclectic group made her smile, and wonder if she was the only one who had an FBI agent, a police captain and a criminal coming to the same party for a little girl turning one.

"What are you smiling at?" Lainey loved seeing Eve smile.

Eve handed Lainey the list, and knew she saw the same oddness.

"Well, it will certainly be an interesting first birthday party," Lainey giggled.

"Maybe I should rethink this whole thing, and have a simple little get together with you, Jack and the boys," Eve teased.

"I believe you've already given the deposit for the ponies."

Eve laughed, but Lainey was actually right. Yes, she hired ponies. So incredibly silly, she knew, but she did it nonetheless. Adam didn't even try to talk her out of it. Eve thought he secretly wanted the ponies for his little girl, too. Hell, he wanted everything for his little princess, which is exactly why he agreed to buying her a tiny tiara.

"You think I overdid it on the party."

"No."

"You should work on that, Lainey. It was not convincing at all." Eve winked at her, tapping her on the nose before walking past her.

Lainey watched Eve post the guest list on the refrigerator, and couldn't help but smile at the "art work" that also took up residence there. Bella may be one, but she was certainly Eve's daughter. Those finger paintings had the makings of masterpieces. Of course, Lainey was probably as biased as Eve was when it came to Bella, but that didn't detract from the cuteness of the little drawings.

Lainey was also a little surprised by the amount of things on Eve's fridge. Everything had always been so neat, so pristine when it came to Eve, that seeing a bit of chaos was just odd—and endearing. It made Lainey's heart beat a little faster for Eve. Crap.

"What are you thinking about?"

Lainey cleared her throat, thinking quick about how to answer.

"Um. How long do you think it will take to get back to the gallery?"

Eve eyed Lainey. That was certainly not what she was thinking, but since they weren't alone, Eve wouldn't push it.

"I don't know. I'll get in touch with Charlie later. Then, I'll call James and see what he has to say."

"It's killing you, not being there isn't it?"

"It's killing me to stand by and do nothing. But, I have more to lose now."

"How long will you stay away?"

Eve thought about Adam. He, of course, would want her to stay away until some kind of progress is made. But, she didn't know if she could do that. The gallery was her baby. She wouldn't let it be taken away from her again.

"I'll talk it over with Adam." Lainey's look of surprise made Eve smile. "I'm working on it, Lainey."

Eve sat in bed, leaning forward to rub lotion on her legs. She turned her head just in time to see Adam walk out of the bathroom dressed in black pajama pants that rode low on his hips. He was shirtless, and Eve couldn't keep her eyes from trailing down his six-pack, down to that perfect V dipping into the bottoms. She breathed in through her nose, and could smell the crisp scent of him. Setting her lotion on the bedside table, she crooked her finger at him.

Adam grinned. His grin broadened when Eve changed positions, laying propped up on her elbows, with her legs towards him, spread. She was wearing one of his white t-shirts and white panties. He didn't think she could be any sexier. Well, maybe if she were completely naked, which he had every intention of making happen. Soon.

He climbed the platform to her, bending to kiss her from her thigh to her belly button. Adam pushed the shirt up over her breasts, taking a nipple between his teeth.

Eve moaned in response, threading her fingers through his hair to hold him there.

"You're beautiful," he murmured, nuzzling his cheek to her breast. He moved up, feathering kisses on her neck, tugging her earlobe into his mouth. "*I love you.*"

The words were just a breath in her ear, but they burned a trail straight to her heart. "*I love you, baby.*" She turned her head to meet his lips in tender kiss. Their tongues touched, and Eve felt herself melt into him. He was being gentle with her. In the back of her mind, she wondered if it was because of what happened the night before. But, when he lifted her arms above her head, pushing her shirt up until she was free of it, she forgot everything else.

He got up on his knees, hooking two fingers into her panties, he slid them down over her hips. She raised her legs in front of him, to assist him. After throwing them to the floor, he traced his hands from the inside of her ankles, down, spreading her legs as he went.

She used her toes to grab onto Adam's pajama bottoms, and tugged at them. "Take them off, baby."

"Soon."

He dipped his head to taste her, but she stopped him by grasping his face in her hands. Her eyes fixed on his.

"I want you inside me, Adam. I need to feel you."

He saw the raw need burning in her gaze, and wanted nothing more than to give her everything. In a quick motion, the bottoms were discarded, and he moved between her legs. Adam put a hand between them, touching her.

"You're so wet, beautiful. So ready for me."

"I'm always ready for you, Adam." Eve wrapped her hand around his thick cock and guided it to her opening. Even though Adam was large, and it always took Eve a moment to accommodate his size, she felt their bodies were made for each other. That feeling became stronger when he slipped inside her, filling her completely.

Even as she gasped at the invasion, her hands grabbed his ass, and pulled him deeper.

"All the way, *amant*. More."

He obliged, shifting his hips until he was buried inside her to the root. He supported his weight on his left elbow, taking Eve's leg with his right and wrapping it around him. Adam looked into Eve's eyes, and began to move slowly.

"You feel incredible, Eve."

She tightened around him in response. Their eyes never left each other as she matched his rhythm, her breath hitching with pure, unadulterated love. Eve heard Adam's breath quicken, and she moved her hips faster, feeling the pressure build in herself. She was close and wanted Adam to go over with her.

"Adam!"

Adam rolled his hips, making her cry out in pure ecstasy. She didn't know how much longer she could hold on, but she knew he was close. Eve felt his body tighten, each muscle tense with the need to release. It made her so hot, she was on the edge of the spectacular orgasm when she heard him.

"Tell me, beautiful!"

Eve knew exactly what he wanted to hear and she gave it to him without hesitation.

"I'm coming, Adam! Oh, God, I'm coming, baby!"

His answering growl was more than enough to push her over into unimaginable pleasure, and he emptied inside her with his own explosive orgasm.

Their still ragged breath mingled together as they kissed each other with a mix of satisfaction, and an insatiable need for one another that seemed to never go away.

Eve smiled against his lips when he moved inside her. She loved when he did that. It meant he wanted to stay inside her for as long as she would allow him to. Seriously, if she could get away with it, she would allow him to be there always.

Eve took his face in her hands, caressing his cheeks with her thumbs.

"Let's go away." She hadn't meant to say those words, but there they were. And, there was no taking them back now.

Adam's body stilled, and he searched her face.

"Where do you want to go?" He had the Griffen account, and was in the process of figuring out how to make the transition to his own firm. But, Eve rarely asked for anything from him, and he was determined to give her whatever she needed.

Eve's lips curved into a half smile. "I have no idea. I didn't even know I was going to say that."

Adam rolled off Eve, bringing her to him to rest on his chest. "Is this something you need, beautiful?"

She pressed her cheek to his chest, and sighed. "I think it's something both of us need." Eve raised her head to look at him again. "I should have told you what happened immediately. I'm sorry I didn't."

"I understand." Adam pushed a strand of hair out of Eve's face, and tucked it behind her ear. "You still think I'm going to blow up one day?"

"No." She grinned, and winked at him. "But, I'd like to make sure that it doesn't happen by doing everything I can to let you know how sorry I am."

"Tonight was definitely a great start at that."

Eve had surprised him with a beautiful dinner that consisted of petit filet mignon and a broiled lobster tail paired with grilled asparagus with Hollandaise and Truffle-Reggiano fries. When she added an amazing merlot imported from Italy, it was heaven. After dinner, they played with Bella, bathed her together and watched TV until it was Bella's bedtime. All of that, topped off by making love to the most beautiful woman he's ever seen? How could he possibly hold on to any anger towards her.

"I could do more."

"Oh, I know." Adam's smirk made Eve laugh. He took a deep breath, then blew it out in frustration. "But, I just don't think I can get away right now, beautiful."

"I know you're busy, baby. But, what if it were just a couple of days?" Eve sat up abruptly. "I know where I want to go."

"Tell me." Adam bent an arm behind his head to prop it up.

"Los Angeles."

Adam chuckled. "Really? You could pick anywhere to go, and you choose LA?"

"Yes!" Eve bounced to her knees, causing her tits to bounce and catch Adam's attention. Eve snapped her fingers in front of his face. "Hey. Eyes on me, pal."

"They are on you. Believe me."

Eve shook her head with a laugh. With a finger to his chin, she pressed up until he looked at her face.

"Pay attention."

"I was."

His boyish grin became a full on smile when she raised a brow at him.

"I'm listening! I swear. But, you gotta know, beautiful, that it's extremely hard to concentrate when you're naked in front of me." The gleam in his eye was wicked. "Extremely *hard*."

Eve glanced down at his impressive hard on, and her mouth began to water.

"Hmm. Well, I will get right on that. *After*, you listen to me."

"All ears." Adam grinned and wiggled his eyebrows at Eve.

"You're impossible." She straddled his torso, planting her hands on either side of his head. "I want to open a gallery in LA. And, I want you to design it."

Adam's eyes—which were fixated on her breasts again—snapped up. "What?"

"Got your attention now, don't I? I want to be one of the first clients of your new firm. Sumptor Gallery, LA. I've always wanted to open a gallery there, but haven't gotten around to it. I think now is the perfect time."

"When someone is vandalizing this one?"

A shadow crossed Eve's face making Adam curse.

"I'm sorry ..."

Eve pressed a finger to Adam's lips. "Hush. And, yes. You would prefer that I stay away from the gallery for now, and I respect that. This would give me something to focus on without going insane."

"You're serious about this?"

"Yes. I can scope out some places online tomorrow, make some appointments, and Saturday, after Bella's party, we can fly out there and take a look." She leaned down and brushed her lips against Adam's. "If you need to be back before Monday, we can make that work."

"Okay, baby. If this is something you want, we'll do it. But, you can't hire me. I'm your husband. I do things for you."

"Unh uh, nope." Eve shook her head. "I hire your firm."

"I don't even have a firm yet, beautiful."

"But, you will soon. And, Sumptor, Inc. will hire you to design the gallery."

He saw the determined set of her jaw, and knew there was no arguing with her. "Whatever you want, beautiful." Adam shifted his hips to remind her there was another pressing topic that needed to be addressed.

Eve got the hint, and as promised, got right on that.

Chapter Nine

"What are you looking at?" Lainey bent over Eve's shoulder, and peered at the computer screen. She saw Eve was on a real estate site, and frowned. "Are you moving?"

Eve shifted until she was face to face with Lainey.

"And, leave you? Of course not." She smiled at the slight flush that crept up Lainey's neck. "I'm looking for space for a new gallery."

"I don't understand. You want to move the gallery?"

"No. I'm going to open a new one. In Los Angeles."

"Oh! I think that's wonderful!"

"Yeah?"

Lainey grinned at Eve. She enjoyed the fact that Eve still thought Lainey's opinions were important.

"I've actually wondered why it's taken you so long to open one there."

Eve turned back to the computer, and clicked on a property that interested her. "I had planned on it, but then the fire happened. I put all of my focus on reopening here."

"Do you think this is the best time to open a new gallery with everything going on?"

Eve shrugged. "Like I told Adam, it'll give me something to keep me occupied. Charlie hasn't found any leads, yet, as to who killed Branson. Even James is hitting a roadblock. If I don't get my mind on something else, I'm going to get in trouble with Adam."

"You really are trying hard for him," Lainey laughed. "I think that's sweet."

"You think everything is sweet," Eve mumbled teasingly.

"Eve, you have changed so much these past couple of years. Letting Adam be there for you, and being a mother has been really good for you." Lainey laid a hand on Eve's shoulder. "It makes me happy to see that."

Eve patted Lainey's hand. "Sit down with me. I want to get your feedback on some of these places."

Lainey pulled a chair close to Eve. Yes, she may have breathed in Eve's scent as she sat down, but Lainey refused to believe that wasn't normal.

Eve hid her knowing smile. Lainey was back to being an open book, and Eve enjoyed it. Flirting wasn't bad, as long as you didn't act on it. Right?

"Oh, that one is nice." Lainey pointed out a property that Eve had been particularly drawn to as well. "Is it set up to be a gallery?"

"No. I think it actually used to be a restaurant. But, Adam will be doing the redesign." Eve Googled the area, and came across some reviews of surrounding businesses. "Seems like a good area. A florist, a diner and even a wine bar are in the same little strip. Sounds good, right?"

"Sure. The patrons will have options for a great night out, with great art to finish the date. What could be better?"

"You certainly have a positive outlook on this."

"Hey, as long as you're not moving to LA, I'm all for a new gallery. Sharing art with the world is a great thing." Lainey picked up her cooling coffee, and sat back. "When are you going to see the properties?"

"After Bella's party."

"That soon?"

"I figured it would be good for Adam and me."

Lainey made a small sound into her coffee cup that she didn't think Eve heard.

"Problem?"

"Hmm? No." Lainey sighed. "I'm seriously trying to get over this damn jealousy thing, Eve. I feel so bipolar sometimes. One minute, I'm wanting nothing but happiness for you and Adam. The next, I'm wishing it was back to the way it was when we were together. It's not fair to you, or to Jack. Maybe being away from you for a little bit will help."

Eve couldn't help being hurt by that, but she understood. "We're only going to be gone for a day, Lainey. Don't get too excited."

"I didn't mean that the way it sounded, Eve."

"Yes, you did. But, it's okay. I get it." Eve printed the info on the screen and stood up. "Come on. We have a party to get ready for."

He was taking a chance, being so close. He just didn't care. The bitch was getting ready to give that little girl of hers a party. He watched the little girl running around with her nanny, laughing. So happy. He wondered what Eve would do if she lost her. He would see. The police are running around in circles, trying to find clues, but he's not a moron, like Eve's father was. He knew who to hire, and how to keep himself out of it. He turned his attention back to Eve, who was smiling at her little girl, and putting up decorations. It surprised him that the vandalism at the gallery didn't upset Eve as much as he had anticipated. Perhaps it was time for the next step.

"Happy birthday, my sweet little girl." Eve picked Bella up out of her crib, and kissed her on both cheeks. She hugged her close, closing her eyes. "*You are my soul, baby girl.*"

Eve thought of the locket her mother left her, with the engraving "Two bodies, One soul". She would pass that locket down to Bella one day, and the thought brought tears to her eyes.

Adam stood at the door, silently watching them together. The love he felt radiating from Eve, the love he felt for both of them, left him breathless. Unable to stay away any longer, he went to them, wrapping his arms around them.

"My two favorite girls," he said softly, burrowing his face into Eve's neck. "Is our little princess ready for her big day?"

Eve smiled. "She will be, daddy. We're just going to freshen up, then we'll put on something pretty, and she'll be ready to welcome everyone."

"She'll be the prettiest little girl there." Adam kissed Bella on the cheek, then turned to Eve. "And, her momma will be the most beautiful woman." He leaned in and brushed his lips over Eve's.

Eve and Adam's backyard was filled with people celebrating Bella's birthday. The birthday girl was dressed like her momma, both wearing white shorts, with a white tank. Eve knew it probably wasn't the best choice for Bella, with the cake, the ponies, and all the playing around, but she couldn't help it. Her little girl just looked so cute! Add the tiny tiara, and Eve wanted nothing more than to keep snapping photos.

There was good food, good music and, believe it or not, good conversation. If she didn't see it herself, Eve would not have believed it was possible that such a diverse group would be so accepting of each other.

The kids were kept occupied by riding ponies, having a grand time. Lainey had been hijacked by Trudy, talking about having their boys spend more time together. Adam huddled with James, Charlie and Billy—when he wasn't with Eve—but assured her they weren't talking over Eve's case. She didn't want what was happening to affect today.

Everyone else just seemed to mingle, or watch the kids. What mattered the most to Eve was that everyone was laughing and having fun. With the sun shining, and the beautiful weather, it was turning out to be the perfect day.

"Eve?"

Lexie's hesitant voice cut through Eve's pleasant thoughts.

"Yes?"

"Um, I'm sure you didn't mean to keep your studio unlocked, but Hunter ..."

Eve frowned. "Lexie, I don't leave my studio unlocked." With the art and photos that she had in the studio, Eve knew better than to leave the door open for curious little ones to be able to explore.

"Oh. Then I'm not sure how Hunter got these." Lexie blushed, and handed her provocative photos Eve had taken of herself and Adam. She had been trying her hand at self-portraits, and succeeded quite well. Seeing them in Lexie's hand was definitely *not* what Eve had planned for those photos.

"Oh my god." Eve snatched the photos from Lexie. "Keep an eye on Bella, please."

Eve walked briskly towards her studio. She didn't want to draw any unwanted attention, so she kept a smile on her face, greeting her guests cheerfully as she walked by. There was no way she left the studio unlocked. It was just so unlike her to do something like that. If she had, the only explanation she could come up with as to why, was the stress of the past few days must've affected her more than she thought.

Sure enough, the door to Eve's studio was ajar when she got there. Damn it! She hated being so careless, especially on a day like today. She pushed her way in, and stopped dead in her tracks.

Photos were scattered all over the floor, and her paintings were ransacked as though someone had been looking for something. When her eye caught the portrait she had painted of Adam, her heart stopped. A knife protruded from Adam's illustrated chest. She was so focused on that, she almost didn't notice the word "WHORE" painted in red across the far wall.

"What do you want from me!" Eve didn't realize she had screamed the words until Adam ran into the studio.

"Eve!" When he heard Eve scream, fear made his blood run cold. Finding her standing in the middle of the chaos in her studio, lit a fire of rage in his belly. "My God."

Eve's outburst brought the attention she didn't want as person after person filed in, with Charlie pushing his way ahead of everyone else.

Eve couldn't hear what Charlie was saying over the ringing in her ears. All she could feel was people surrounding her, seeing her in one of her most vulnerable moments.

"Get them out."

"Baby, let Harris …"

"Get them out, Adam. Now!"

Adam could hear Eve's patience slipping fast, so he began ushering everyone out. He caught Lainey's eye, and she nodded discreetly.

"Adam, I need to get in there and start documenting this."

"Not now, Harris. Let Eve have some space for a minute."

Lainey waited until everyone was out, then went to Eve and wrapped her arms around her.

"Lainey, please go."

The words bit into Lainey's ego, but she held on tighter when Eve tried to break the embrace.

"I'm here, honey."

"I need to be alone."

"No. You need to be around people who love you. Stop fighting it, and let go." She felt Eve's body begin to shake with silent sobs, and fought to keep her own composure.

Lainey was soon aware of Adam's hand on her shoulder, and she gently shifted Eve into his arms.

"Could you watch Bella while Lexie packs a few things for her?" Adam asked Lainey, softly. "We're going to leave earlier than expected."

"Of course. And, I'll make sure everyone gets out okay."

Adam mouthed his 'thank you' and turned his attention to his wife. He stayed quiet, sensing what Eve needed was just the strength of his arms, not his words. There was nothing he could say, anyway. Everything he had in his head held contempt and anger for whoever was doing this to her, anyway. That wouldn't help the situation.

"Why are they doing this to me?"

"Harris, James and Donovan will figure this out, beautiful. You, Bella and I are getting away for a couple of days."

Eve sighed. "How can I go now? I have to find out who's doing this ..."

"That's not your job, Eve. Let Harris handle it."

Eve stepped away from him and wiped the tears from her eyes. Fury was quickly taking the place of her distress. She marched to the painting of Adam.

"Do you see this?" Eve pointed angrily at the knife. "This is a threat against *you*! Do you think I'm going to stand by while they threaten my *husband*?"

"Baby, look around you. It's not just a threat to me, it's a threat to *us*. For all we know, Bella could be included in that! We are getting out of here, and we're doing it now."

"Adam ..."

"Not up for discussion, Eve. Pack a few things, and let the authorities do what they have to do."

Eve raised a brow. Either those around her are getting much more comfortable speaking to her in a way she wasn't accustomed to, or she was losing her authoritative edge. Either way, she heard the firm resolve in Adam's voice. So, she did what any woman would do. She changed tactics.

"There are things in here that I don't want others to see, *amant*. Things I don't think you want others to see. Particularly Billy."

"Nice try, beautiful, but we're going. I'll talk to Harris and tell him he needs to be discreet. I'll even talk to Lainey, and see if she can be here while they're here."

Even though she still wanted to be here to find out who was threatening her family, Eve knew she couldn't argue with him. It made her feel a little better knowing Lainey would be here.

"Fine." She went to him, and caressed his cheek. "You owe me for talking to me the way you did."

Adam's lips curved slightly. "You can take it out on me later."

Chapter Ten

Everything okay?

It was probably the twentieth text Eve had sent Lainey, but she couldn't help herself. To Lainey's credit, she wasted no time replying.

Still fine. Try 2 relax.

Fat chance of that, Eve thought to herself. Adam was on the couch of their private jet with a fussy Bella. She had already tried calming Bella down, but the little one just didn't like to fly apparently. When nothing Eve was doing was helping, Adam took over, without much success. She turned back to her phone, and texted Lainey, again.

Are they still there?

Eve's phone chimed a few moments later.

Yes. Charlie won't let anyone in the studio unless they absolutely need to be. I'm here, and I'll be here until they leave.

Eve thanked Lainey, promising her she wouldn't keep bombarding her with texts. She put her phone away, and joined Adam and Bella.

"Did you decide to give Lainey a break?"

Eve's eyes cut to Adam. "You're already in trouble, pal. Do you really want to make it worse?"

"I don't know. Will spanking be involved?"

"You are incorrigible," Eve laughed. "But, yes, spanking will definitely be involved."

Adam's crystal blue eyes darkened with desire. "Don't promise something you're not going to go through with."

Eve leaned closer. "Have you ever known me to back down on anything?" With a wink, Eve plucked Bella out of Adam's arms, and got up to walk around with her, bouncing her on her hip.

Adam watched Eve closely. He knew she was trying to cover up the fact that she had fear and anger just below the surface, but he saw it. Her body almost vibrated with it. If he could do anything to help get her mind off of what was going on back home, he would do it, whatever it cost him.

∞

Adam pushed Eve's hair from her face, using the quiet moment to study her sleeping features. It was times like this, when she was peaceful, that her youth came through. He could forget most days that she hadn't even turned thirty yet, except when he watched her sleep. He almost didn't want to rouse her.

"Wake up, beautiful."

Eve groaned, burying her face deeper in the pillow. "I already sexed you up, pal. Leave me alone."

Her muffled words made Adam laugh. After they finally got Bella to sleep, Eve certainly kept her word and 'punished' him. And, oh, how amazing it was.

"We're here, Eve. Up." Adam emphasized the last word with a sound smack on Eve's bare ass.

She jolted and shot him a snarky look before dropping her head back to the pillow.

"We land in less than ten, beautiful. Up and at 'em."

"Okay, okay. I'm getting up. Sheesh, you're so bossy."

Adam leaned close to her ear. "You know you love it when I'm bossy." It was a variation of their usual, playful banter when she was being particularly cranky. One he enjoyed a great deal. Adam kissed the small of her back, rolling his tongue down just enough to tease her, and then left her wanting more.

∞

They walked hand in hand on the sidewalk of the tree-lined, quaint little street that boasted a diversified bunch of small, attractive shops. It was exactly as advertised when Eve found the area online. A small gallery would fit in perfectly here.

Bella babbled contentedly in her BabyBjorn strapped to Adam's chest. She seemed to like it here, or perhaps she was just glad she wasn't on the plane anymore. Whatever the reason, Eve savored the smiles Bella gave her. To everyone on the street that passed them, they looked to be a happy little family without a care in the world. Eve was determined to feel that way while she was here. She even cut back on texting Lainey for information. A little.

"Are you hungry, baby?" Eve glanced up at Adam, seeing him take in his surroundings with an architect's eye.

"Hmm?" He had been distracted with the beauty of the architecture, thinking of how he would design Eve's gallery to flow with the construction here.

Eve stopped in front of a diner with pretty iron chairs and tables out front. "Let's grab something to eat here before we look at the property. I'm hungry, and I'm sure Bella could eat."

"Sounds good."

Eve was finding the people to be just as nice as the surroundings, which made her decision to buy here even easier. The owner of the diner, Ellie, had all of the charm of a small town girl, and their waitress, Ellie's daughter, followed in her mom's footsteps—no small feat for being a teenager.

After lunch, they continued their stroll, checking everything out at a leisurely pace. Eve paused in front of a seemingly unassuming flower shop. "Do you mind?"

Adam was enjoying the afternoon with Eve and Bella so much, that if she had asked him to shoe shop with her, he'd probably say yes. Okay, maybe he wouldn't go that far, but a flower shop isn't so bad. He tipped his chin, and opened the door.

Before Eve could step inside, a raven haired young girl stepped out, locking eyes with Eve.

"Excuse me. I am sorry." The girl's voice held a bewitching English accent, but it was her eyes that intrigued Eve the most. They were almost translucent, and Eve wished then that she had thought to bring her Nikon with her. She smiled at the girl, letting her pass, and letting her photographic memory take in the features so she could at least paint her later.

"I wish I had brought my camera," she heard herself mumble to Adam.

Adam's response was preempted by yet another accented voice.

"It was her eyes, wasn't it?" the woman asked Eve. "I deal with beauty every day, and I've never seen anything like them." She smiled sheepishly at Eve. "I'm sorry, I wasn't trying to eavesdrop. I'm Blaise Knight. I own this shop."

Eve cocked a brow, and shook Blaise's outstretched hand. And, for the second time wished she'd had her camera. With such beautiful people around, the artist in her was working overtime.

"What an interesting name," Eve replied with a grin. "Eve Riley. This is my husband Adam, and our daughter Bella."

Adam nodded his greeting, while Blaise gushed over Bella.

"Oh, she is precious!" In an abrupt movement, Blaise turned on her heel, motioning for them to follow her. "What can I help you with?"

Eve's brows drew together. "I'm trying to detect your accent. Australian?"

"Kiwi," Blaise smiled. "I'm from New Zealand."

"Blaise?" A man walked up that almost gave Adam a run for his money in the looks department. Not quite, in Eve's mind, but very close.

"I'm busy, Mr. Steele." Eve noted that Blaise's attitude cooled a good amount. "I have customers."

"Fine. I'll be back." The man nodded in Eve and Adam's direction and took off.

"Sorry about that."

Eve chuckled. It was certainly interesting around here. "Not a problem. I'm actually looking into buying the establishment next door, so I thought I'd stop in and get to know the neighbors."

"Oh? That's fantastic! Unless you're planning on opening a flower shop."

That extracted another laugh from Eve, as well as Adam.

"No, though I do deal with beauty, as well. It will be an art gallery."

"Now, that *is* fantastic news. I love art."

Eve took a moment to look around the shop. The flowers were exquisite, and unlike anything she'd seen before. "Your flowers are quite beautiful. I would love for you to do the arrangements when we open."

"Really? I would be honored! Let me get some information from you, and give you my card. We'll get everything set for when you need us."

Eve followed Blaise to the counter, glancing back at Adam who was pointing out pretty flowers to Bella.

"What will the name of the gallery be?"

"Sumptor Gallery, LA."

"Oh my god, you're Eve Sumptor? I thought you looked vaguely familiar. I've been to some of your galleries. They're absolutely amazing!"

"Thank you."

They exchanged information, and a few more pleasantries before Eve and Adam left.

"Friendly people."

Eve smiled up at Adam. "Yes. Almost makes you want to think about moving here and forgetting all of the shit happening at home."

"Could you do that?" Adam was more than a little surprised by that.

Eve hesitated for only a moment. "No. I'd miss New York too much." And Lainey, Eve added silently. "But, it's nice to know we have options."

∞

The rest of the day was spent scoping out the property, and talking about all of the possibilities. After discussing it with Adam, Eve made an offer on the place. Since her offer was so generous, it was instantly accepted, much to Eve's delight. She was actually looking forward to working closely with Adam on the design. Of course, the fact that she found Adam to be extremely sexy when he was in work mode was an added bonus.

Eve spent a little time getting in touch with her contacts to let them know she would be opening a new gallery. They were happy, obviously, knowing the business Sumptor Galleries bring in.

Adam was also on the phone a lot, putting out fires or making last minute changes. He was ready to make the break from the firm. There was just too much mirco-managing for him, and he'd be much happier not having to deal with the politics anymore. As it were, he had no other choice but to get back to New York immediately. Something he was actually dreading since Eve seemed to be more at peace here, away from all that was going on.

Dragging his heels, he left the office of the suite they had booked, to look for Eve. She was feeding Bella a snack when he found her.

"Hey beautiful."

"Hey gorgeous." Eve glanced up at him with a smile, that faded when she saw his expression. Instantly alert, and scared something may have happened to Lainey, Eve's pulse started racing. "What's wrong?"

Adam noticed the fear in Eve's eyes. "No, nothing's wrong. Nothing like what you're thinking," he said quickly. "I just have to get back sooner than we intended."

Eve drew in a deep breath. This shit was really getting to her and she hated it. If Charlie and the others didn't come up with solutions soon, she was going to go crazy. "Oh. That's fine. I knew coming out here it was going to be a short trip."

Eve said she was fine with it, but, in reality, she was torn. It had been easy for her to forget, even just a little, about the threats against her and her family. Going back meant having to face it all.

Did she have the strength to do that? If it meant saving Adam and Bella, Eve would find the strength, no matter what she had to do.

Chapter Eleven

Lainey found Eve standing in her studio, her hands on her hips, just taking everything in. She was dressed in jeans and a t-shirt, her feet bare, and her hair up in a ponytail. So young, Lainey thought sadly. She's been through so much in her life, it isn't fair she has to go through more.

"Eve, honey?"

"Did you cover it?" Eve asked without turning around.

"I'm sorry?"

"The word on the wall. Did you cover it?"

Damn. Lainey had hoped that Eve hadn't seen that awful word. She had been so focused, and rightfully so, on Adam's portrait and the threat it insinuated. Lainey should have known that Eve's sharp eyes would see everything.

"I didn't think you should have to deal with it. I cleaned up as much as I could after the crime scene guys left."

"*Thank you.*"

The words were whispered, and Lainey could feel the emotion in them so deep, it rocked her.

"I took inventory. I don't know how you keep track of what you have here in your personal studio." Lainey handed Eve the folder she brought with her. "But, I thought it would be easier for you to see if something was missing if I wrote it all down."

Eve looked down at the folder with puzzlement.

"You took inventory?"

"Yes. I just …"

Eve surprised Lainey by taking her in her arms and holding tight.

"*I don't know how else to express my gratitude to you,*" Eve whispered close to Lainey's ear. She pressed her lips to Lainey's cheek, letting them linger. Backing away slowly, she laid her forehead on Lainey's. She wanted to kiss Lainey, and she didn't want to want it. Her life never could be uncomplicated, could it?

"*Eve.*" God, she wanted Eve to kiss her. But, with the way things were, she didn't know if Eve would do it because she needed it, too, or if she just felt grateful enough to do it.

"Just give me a second, Lainey. Please?"

Lainey's eyes fluttered shut when she felt Eve wrap a strand of hair around her finger. With a sigh, Eve finally backed away. Lainey took the silent moment Eve gave her when she opened the folder to study the list, and caught her breath, steadying herself.

"You catalogued everything?" Eve flipped through several pages in awe.

"Well, not quite everything. I didn't do the stuff in your back room."

Eve's most personal creations were in that back room, and it stayed locked unless she absolutely needed to get in there.

"I did check to see if anything in there had been disturbed," Lainey continued, nervously. "But, I had to unlock it, and it looked like everything was in its place. I'm sorry I went in there …"

"Lainey, stop. I gave you a key. You're more than welcome to go in there. I'm glad nothing else was ruined …" Eve's voice trailed off as she remembered the knife sticking out of Adam. No, his painting, Eve corrected her thoughts. You will not let anything happen to him. Damn, she wished she could believe the optimistic voice in her head.

"I was surprised to see Adam's portrait out here. I thought you usually keep that inside the back room. That's why I checked it."

Eve looked up, and held Lainey's eyes. "I was going to frame it." She lifted a shoulder in a small shrug. "I wanted to hang it up out here."

"I see."

"I'm going to frame yours, too, Lainey."

"You're not going to hang it up out here!"

"No, of course not." Eve let out a small laugh when Lainey breathed a sigh of relief.

"Does Adam know about it?"

"No. I did manage to keep a few secrets." Eve's eyes lowered, almost shamefully, but Lainey didn't catch the expression, or read it wrong for she said nothing.

They were comfortably silent for a while as Eve read through Lainey's list. She didn't readily notice anything missing, which, to her, meant this was very personal. Eve rarely sold her own work, so when she did, they were worth quite a bit. If whomever broke in here knew that, something would certainly have been taken. So, this had definitely been a threat. But, why? And, who? Eve was busy contemplating this when she noticed Lainey shifting nervously.

"Lainey? Is something wrong?"

Lainey opened her mouth to say something, then closed it. After a few more attempts, she blew out a frustrated breath.

Eve just watched in silent amusement. When they were together Lainey had been understandably nervous. If she were unsure about what to do, how to act or what to say, she would fidget, and a slight flush would creep up her neck. Eve enjoyed it then as much as she did now.

"Stop laughing at me."

"I'm not laughing." Eve smiled slightly, then hesitated. Before, she would distract Lainey with kisses, or touches in all the right places until Lainey was bold enough to say what she wanted. Eve couldn't do that now, so she set the folder aside and clasped her hands in front of her. "Talk to me."

"I wanted to ask you a question," Lainey said in a rush.

Eve arched a perfect brow questioningly, and waited.

Lainey swallowed hard, squared her shoulders and went for it. "How long have you known you were … bisexual?"

The laugh that escaped Eve's mouth made Lainey frown, and Eve cursed silently. "I'm sorry, Lainey. I don't mean to laugh. It's just, your question caught me off guard."

"Do you know how long it took me to get the courage to ask you that question?"

"Two years?" Eve teased, and grabbed Lainey's arm before she could get up and stomp out. "Sorry. To answer your question, I don't think I'm bisexual."

Lainey's brows furrowed. "But, you're ... attracted to women," she said quietly, as though someone would hear her.

"I'm not attracted to women, Lainey. I'm attracted to *you*."

Not past tense, Lainey thought, headily. It didn't mean anything would happen, but she still felt good about it. Still, she didn't know if she understood. Of course, Eve was the only woman Lainey had been attracted to, but ...

Eve stared at Lainey, wondering what exactly was going on in that pretty head of hers. She could imagine some of it, and went on to try to explain.

"I'm an artist, honey. I can see beauty in anything." Eve thought of her father, and what was going on now. "Almost anything," she amended. "I can find women attractive, but I have never been *attracted*. Until you. I didn't fall for you because you were a woman. I fell for you *in spite* of that."

Lainey blinked. She knew Eve loved her, but even so, anytime she heard Eve say her feelings out loud, it had the same devastating effect on her.

The breath Lainey blew out was filled with relief, for reasons Eve couldn't begin to know. She gave Lainey a questioning look, and heard her sigh.

"I have been trying to figure out what is going on with me," Lainey confessed. "I have never been attracted to another woman before. When I met you, I was having problems with Jack, and finding you to be incredibly sexy." Lainey ignored Eve's surprised—and sly—grin. "I didn't know if maybe, somehow, I was ... changing. Hearing how you explain it ... helps."

"You thought you were becoming bisexual?"

"What else could I think? You're a woman, I'm attracted to you. Hell, I *slept* with you." She whispered the word as though it hurt her to say it. "If it's not that, what do I call it?"

"Must you put a label on it?"

"I guess not."

Lainey almost sounded petulant, which made Eve smile. "How about equal opportunist?"

That brought a slight smile to Lainey's lips, which was immediately replaced by a frown.

"Do you think we made a mistake?"

"Choosing not to be with each other?" When Lainey nodded, Eve took a deep breath. "I often wonder what my life would have been like had I chosen you. I don't regret my choice, Lainey. I can't. I love Adam, and I have Bella, whom I also love, desperately. But, what you and I had, what we *have* … that is special. It went way beyond just sex."

Eve paused, and looked around her studio that Lainey took the time to clean. She peered at the wall that held the ugly word, which was now as pristine as it was before.

"No one else would have thought to do this for me," she told Lainey quietly, gesturing around her. "Adam is more of the must-keep-my-woman-safe type. He will stand by me, fight for me, and I love that about him. I'm not saying you wouldn't do that for me," she said quickly when Lainey looked hurt. "I'm saying *this*," Eve tapped the folder, "must have taken you hours to do. And, you did it because you thought it would help me. Not only here in the studio, but here." Eve placed her hand over her heart. "*That's* why you are who you are to me."

Eve stood, and held her hand out to Lainey. When Lainey took it, Eve pulled her close.

"I don't think we made a mistake, Lainey. But ..."

She watched as Lainey closed her eyes on the 'but'. Without much thought, but being motivated purely by feeling, Eve cupped Lainey's cheek and leaned in. Their lips were a breath apart, and Eve felt Lainey tremble as Eve's other hand came to rest on Lainey's hip.

The shrill of Eve's phone made them both jump, just as their lips were about to touch.

"*Shit.*" What in the hell had she been thinking. Oh, right. She wasn't thinking. Eve chastised herself for doing that to Lainey, to Adam ... even to herself. She could do nothing more than push it aside now as she took her phone out of her pocket. "It's James," Eve told Lainey before answering.

Lainey's heart continued to pound in her chest. It sounded so loud to her, she was surprised Eve couldn't hear it. What in the hell just happened? She was certain that Eve would have kissed her if the phone hadn't interrupted them. Lainey mentally shook herself. It was only because of what she had done for Eve, and she was just feeling particularly emotional, and grateful, and caught up in the moment. It meant nothing. Lainey kept telling herself that as she listened to Eve talk to James.

"Eve, we need to talk."

"You have information?"

"I have something. Can you meet me at the diner near your gallery?"

Eve paused. Adam wouldn't like her being so close to the gallery, but if it meant finding *something* that could make all of this end, he would have to deal with it. "When?"

"Now, if you're available."

"I'll meet there as soon as I can."

She ended the call, and stood there for a moment before looking at Lainey. She looked as confused and scared as Eve felt. She went to her, and took both of her hands in hers. "Do you want me to apologize?"

Lainey shook her head. God, no, she didn't want to hear an apology from Eve. It may have made her head spin, but she wouldn't complain about it. Except maybe to complain that it was stopped.

"I have to meet James. Do you want to go with me?"

Lainey, still unable to trust her voice, nodded. Eve smiled before pulling her into a soft embrace, and giving her a quick kiss on the cheek.

Eve needed to tell Lexie they were leaving, so they walked to the house together in silence. Neither of them knew what to say anyway. Despite what had just went on in the studio, there wasn't any discomfort between them, and Eve was pleased by that.

They found Lexie feeding Bella lunch in the kitchen.

"Lexie, we have to go out for a bit. Do you think you could stay here with Bella until I get back?"

"Yes, ma'am, of course."

"Don't go anywhere. Stay inside with the doors locked, and don't open the door for anyone. Do you understand?"

Fear flashed across Lexie's face, and Eve was sorry for it. She really had no right to ask Lexie to work for her during this mess. "I know this is a lot to deal with, Lexie. If you're uncomfortable being here, I understand …"

"Eve, I love Bella. And, I enjoy working for you and Mr. Riley. I wish all of this wasn't happening, but I don't want to go anywhere."

"Thank you, Lexie. I won't be long."

―⚮―

Eve strolled into the diner with Lainey, immediately spotting James. He eyed Lainey as they slipped into the booth in front of him.

"Lainey was with me when you called. Whatever you have to say, you can say in front of her."

James shrugged, sipping his coffee.

Eve nodded to the two guys that followed them into the diner. "Yours?"

James shrugged again. "Your husband was insistent that you be watched at all times."

"Adam had you put a detail on me?"

"I would have done it even if he hadn't demanded it. But, he wanted to make sure you were safe. And, he wanted someone on Bella and Lexie if Bella wasn't with you. And, Mrs. Stanton," he finished, jutting his chin up at Lainey.

Both of Eve's brows raised almost enough to meet her hairline. "Adam asked for a detail on Lainey?"

"Mmhmm."

"And, the suit?"

In a casual move, James spied the 'suit' Eve asked about. "Not one of mine. Could be your fed's."

"Billy?" Eve watched James's eyes spark with anger. "What's going on?"

"We have him. We *had* him."

Eve frowned. "Him?"

"The shooter."

Eve lurched forward. "Who is he? Wait, what do you mean you *had* him?"

"Donovan swooped in and took him before we had a chance to ask him anything."

"What does Billy say?"

James laughed mirthlessly. "We haven't heard a damn thing since."

"Why would he do that?"

"He wanted to pull out his dick and show us his was bigger." James glanced at Lainey. "My apologies for the language." He turned back to Eve. "So, he took the shooter, and locked us out. My theory, he wants to solve this and be your hero."

Eve caught herself before she rolled her eyes. "Billy is married, James."

"Marriage never stopped anyone from cheating, Eve."

She felt Lainey stiffen beside her, and discreetly laid a hand on her thigh and squeezed. It was a move made to show solidarity, and Eve was disappointed when Lainey pulled away.

"Well, I have told Billy in no uncertain terms that there would be nothing between us. I'll talk to him, again, and make sure he loops everyone else in."

"Good luck," James muttered. "Dude has a hard on for you, Eve," he continued when she arched a brow. "I guess if he'll listen to anyone, it'll be you."

Eve sighed. "See if you can find out who the suit is."

If Billy was really keeping things from the others, Eve would take care of it. She had enough to deal with between Adam and Lainey. She certainly didn't need more.

"Is it true? About Billy?" Lainey asked as they walked out of the diner.

"That he has a hard on for me?" Eve saw Lainey wince slightly at the words, and nod. "I suppose. He fell for me years ago, when I was younger and he was the rookie FBI agent assigned to me."

"No surprise," Lainey muttered with a smirk. "Do you think he'll listen to you?"

"Who knows. I would have said yes before, but it seems those around me have decided I don't demand the respect I used to."

Lainey detected the mock disappointment in Eve's voice, and at a glance, saw the sly smile. She slipped her arm through Eve's, and laughed.

Chapter Twelve

Lainey's fingers thread through Eve's silken hair as their mouths crushed together. She could feel Lainey push her towards the platform leading to her bed. In the back of her mind, she knew it was wrong, but she couldn't stop.

"*I want to touch you, Eve.*"

A small moan escaped Eve's lips when Lainey lifted Eve's shirt, slipping it over her head, and tossing it to the side. Lainey dipped her head to run her tongue against the exposed skin above the lace of Eve's bra. Eve felt her heart pound, her breathing become heavy, and she knew she was wet and ready.

When she moved her hands over Lainey, she was stopped.

"No, baby. Let me do this for you. Just let go." Lainey gently nudged Eve until she was laying on the bed. With nimble and slightly trembling fingers, Lainey unbuttoned Eve's jeans. Eve lifted her hips to assist Lainey as she slid Eve's jeans and panties down, pitching them to the side with Eve's shirt.

Lainey trailed her fingertips up Eve's smooth legs, over her thighs, and resting right before reaching her sex.

"So beautiful." Lainey got to her knees on the bed in front of Eve. "I've missed you so much." She lowered herself, kissing Eve's toned stomach, and ran her tongue down to that sensitive area of skin that made Eve shiver with pleasure. After a bit of kissing, teasing and nibbling inside Eve's thighs, Lainey finally pressed her tongue to Eve, tasting her. They both groaned with pleasure at the contact, and Eve arched her back, pressing herself harder against Lainey's tongue.

"God, baby! That feels so good!" Her body writhed as Lainey continued her assault by sucking, licking and nibbling Eve's clit. When Lainey slipped her fingers inside her, Eve cried out with the intense thrill that rocked her body. She could feel the pressure building, the need screaming to be released, as she clutched at Lainey's head, holding her close. Her body convulsed as the orgasm swept violently through her.

"Ah!" Eve's eyes flew open as she came, her fingers tugging roughly at the head between her legs. "Adam!" Her heart beat painfully in her chest. Partially from her intense orgasm, and partially from the intense guilt she felt. Fuck!

Adam withdrew his fingers and kissed his way up Eve's body. "Good morning, beautiful." He brought his mouth down to Eve's and kissed her deeply.

Eve could taste herself on Adam's tongue, and it brought on a swirl of new emotions for her. She just couldn't pick one to hold on to, and she hated herself for it. "Good morning," she replied, huskily, hoping her voice didn't betray chaos inside her.

"You sounded as though you were having a really good dream," Adam smiled. "I thought I'd help you out."

Eve's heart stuttered, but she smiled, lacing her fingers behind his head and pulling him to her. *"Dream come true,"* she whispered in his ear. Her smile disappeared when he buried his face in her hair. How could she do this to him? What in the hell was her problem? She was going fucking insane, that's what her problem was, she thought sourly. Staying home and doing nothing was going to be the death of her. Or them.

Adam took one more sniff of her, then sighed. "I have an early meeting. I need to get up and take a shower."

Suddenly, she didn't want to let him go. Eve wanted to show him how much she loved him, and needed him. In a swift move, she reversed their positions, and she straddled him. Without a word, she wrapped her hand around his cock and guided him to her.

"I want this so much, beautiful, but ..."

She covered his mouth with hers, effectively cutting him off, and lowered herself until he was fully sheathed inside her. To make sure he didn't try to pull away again, she moved her body the way she knew he loved. Eve rode him, hard and fast, the need for him consuming her. She braced her arms on the headboard and pushed herself down harder. It still wasn't enough.

"Get on top!"

"Eve ..."

"Now, Adam! I need you to fuck me!"

He heard the desperation in her voice, and quickly flipped them, again, until he had her pinned beneath him. He rammed himself inside her, gaining speed and momentum with each sound she made. He could feel her fingernails dig into his back or ass in an attempt to pull him deeper.

"Fuck me harder, Adam!"

He slammed into her, the need for her growing more and more by the second. Whatever it is she needed, he wanted to give it to her. Their bodies were damp with sweat, and Eve matched each of his thrusts with one of her own. It resulted in loud slaps of naked flesh against naked flesh. The sensual sound made Adam release an animalistic growl as he pounded inside her.

Hurt me! She wanted to yell it to him, beg him, but she kept it inside. Instead, she planted her feet on the bed to push herself into him as he thrust harder, and deeper. It hurt, but not as much as she wanted. Not as much as she needed. The growls and groans of pure pleasure coming from him were so seductive to her that she felt herself at the edge once again.

"Come inside me, baby! Please!"

Her pleas incinerated his control, and his body grew taut. "Ah, *fuck*!" One, two, three more thrusts, and he emptied inside her on an explosive orgasm, calling out her name.

Eve was right there with him, clenching around him as ecstasy took over. The orgasm was so powerful she screamed his name as she came, surprising both of them. She had always been vocal during their lovemaking, but never quite like that.

Adam, his body still tense, his breathing still labored, looked down at her with an arrogant smile. "That was fucking fantastic, baby." He was definitely going to be late for his meeting, but after what she just gave him, he didn't give a damn. He was in no hurry at all as he watched her, completely captivated by the fierce look in her eyes.

"Yes, it was," she replied softly. And, she meant it. It was fantastic. Eve just wished she could stop feeling guilty. It was a dream. She couldn't control her dreams. It was a fucking lame excuse, but she clung to it as if her sanity depended on it.

After a quick shower, Adam left for the office, and Eve, once again, stayed home. In an attempt to be sure Adam saw that she was content with the decision, she told him she would pass some time by looking for offices for his new firm.

Now, more than an hour after he left, the computer was on, and the browser was open, but Eve couldn't focus on a damn thing on the screen. Even the muted sounds of Bella and Lexie in the living room couldn't keep Eve's attention. The stress was getting to her, and for once in her life, she had no clue how to deal with it.

"Eve?" Lainey touched Eve's shoulder gently.

"Shit!" Eve's hand flew to her chest, over her pounding heart. "You scared the hell out of me."

"I'm sorry. I called your name a few times." Lainey sat down next to Eve and searched her face. *Something is off.* "Is everything okay?"

"Mmhmm." Eve tapped a few keys on the computer, until Lainey put her hand on hers.

"Eve..."

Eve carefully pulled her hand away to casually pick up her coffee, offering Lainey a small smile. "I have a lot on my mind, obviously. I must have spaced out for a bit."

Lainey's brows knitted together. *Was she imagining things, or did Eve just pull away from her touch?* She tried shrugging it off, determined not to add to the drama in Eve's life, and focused on the information on the computer screen.

"More real-estate? I thought you bought the place in LA."

"I did. This is for Adam, actually. I'm looking for office space for his new firm." Suddenly, Eve felt an irrational bout of anger. With a grunt, she set her coffee down with a distinct thud, and pushed away from the computer. "This is not me! I'm an artist, not a fucking realtor or secretary!"

The outburst surprised Lainey so much, that she was momentarily frozen. Mentally shaking herself, she stood to join Eve, who was currently standing at the sliding glass door, brooding.

"Eve, honey, talk to me."

"Lainey, I ..." Eve stopped herself. She had been very close to telling Lainey about her dream, and her morning with Adam. "I haven't painted anything since all of this shit started," she said instead, her eyes never leaving the colorful flowers that surrounded her yard. "I just haven't felt inspired."

Lainey knew deep down how awful that was for Eve. Art was something Eve needed, and to have that taken away from her must be horrible. But, Lainey hoped she could make it better somehow. "I would think that's normal with what you're going through. I could pose for you again, if that would help." She had meant it as a joke, but the feral look on Eve's face almost had her taking a step back.

Eve plastered a smile on her face, willing it to look genuine. Lainey couldn't know how her suggestion would affect Eve. But, oh boy, did it affect her. Unable to keep her smile, Eve let it fade. "When you came to work for me, you did it because you had lost yourself. I feel like that's what's happening to me. I have no idea how you did it for twelve years, Lainey. It's only been a few days for me and I feel like I'm going fucking insane."

"You feel like you're not you?" When Eve nodded, Lainey couldn't help but feel sorry for her. She knew exactly what that was like, but honestly, she couldn't imagine Eve surviving like that for long. "Maybe it's because you're not painting."

Eve sighed. "Whatever it is, I feel like I don't know who I am anymore." And, she wanted to kick herself for feeling that way. This was weak—and stupid—and yet, she couldn't stop it.

"You're Adam's wife, Bella's mother … my best friend."

Eve tilted her head sadly. "Everything you just said, Lainey, is who I am to others. Where do I fit in?"

"Eve, if I've learned anything from my experiences with you and my marriage, it's that all of those things are what make you, well, you." Lainey walked to Eve, and touched her lightly on the arm. "But, you're still there. You're still the beautiful, sexy, intelligent and strong woman you've always been."

Images of Eve's dream flashed in her mind then, and she pulled away. "I'm going to the gallery," she announced abruptly.

Concern lit Lainey's eyes. Not only because Eve, once again, pulled away from her, but also for the fact that she was possibly putting herself in danger.

"Are you sure that's a good idea?"

"I *need* to get back to my life, Lainey."

"You have a daughter here. Why can't this be your life?"

A pang of guilt hit Eve in the heart. "Well, if you meant to make me feel like shit, it worked."

"Oh Eve, I didn't mean to make you feel guilty. I just wanted you to see that there's more to you now." Talk about feeling like shit. The last thing Lainey wanted to do is make Eve feel worse, but it seemed like that's all she was doing.

Eve stared at Lainey for a moment before shaking her head. "I love my daughter with everything I am, Lainey. It kills me that being with me at the gallery puts her in danger." She felt the sting of tears, but held them in. "Me staying here, going mad won't be good for her. And, honestly, it won't be good for Adam and me."

Lainey was thrown off balance by Eve's confession. "What do you mean by that?" she asked quietly.

What had she meant? Eve wasn't sure she even knew. It was more of a feeling, and it scared her.

"Nothing. Look, I understand if you can't go to the gallery with me. In fact," she continued before Lainey could respond. "I think it's best if you don't. At least for now."

"Is this the part where you say nasty things to me to keep me away from you and harm?" Lainey didn't even try to hold back the bitterness and hurt. Even after all this time, she still felt the pain of the words Eve said to her. Yes, she may have done it for what she thought were good reasons, but that didn't make Lainey feel any better about it. *"I don't love you. It was sex, it was fun, it was experimental."* God, it had been horrible hearing those words come out of Eve's mouth.

Eve softened. She remembered that time, too. It was the first time since she could remember that she cried. Shit, she did more than sob at the loss of both Lainey and Adam. Eve had allowed herself to fall apart, smoking, drinking, taking pills. She didn't want to go through that ever again. And, she certainly didn't want to put Lainey through that again.

"I've learned my lesson on that," she said softly, and watched Lainey's tense body relax. "I don't want you to stay away from me, Lainey. But, I do need a little time to myself."

Lainey's face fell. She *is* pushing me away, Lainey thought with immense sorrow. "I see."

No, you don't, Eve thought silently. If you did, you wouldn't look as though you lost your best friend. "I'm not pushing you away," she said aloud, and smiled at Lainey's surprise. "I told you. Open book."

"Shit."

Eve genuinely laughed for the first time that day, hugging Lainey lightly. "We're fine, honey. The time alone isn't to get away from you. It's to get back to me."

Eve just hoped she could get back to her before she started hurting the people she loved most.

Chapter Thirteen

Eve had been sitting in her Jag, parked in the garage of her gallery, for the past ten minutes. It was starting to piss her off that she felt such trepidation about being here. And, it wasn't even the danger that made her worry, it was upsetting Adam. She hadn't bothered to call him and tell him she was going to the gallery, figuring the security following her already had instructions to let him know of her whereabouts. Ironically enough, she could feel herself getting pissed about that, as well. Hadn't she done the same when Tony was threatening Adam and Lainey?

She blew out an exasperated breath, laid her head back on the head rest and beat on the steering wheel with her palms. "Come on! Get out of your fucking car and be Eve Sumptor!"

You're not Eve Sumptor, anymore. The thought nagged her until she shut it down. She may not be Eve Sumptor anymore, but the hell if she wasn't still in there.

The elevator opened, and Eve stepped out, drawing in a deep breath. The smell of art had always been relaxing to her. Most people thought she was weird, saying there wasn't a smell. But, oh, there was, and it calmed Eve.

"Mrs. Riley!"

If Eve were the squealing type, this would've been the time to do it. As it were, she let out a sound of surprise, whirling around to find Mikey walking towards her.

"Mikey. If you ever sneak up on me like that again ..." She paused and tried to regulate her breathing and heart rate, holding up her hand to cut off whatever Mikey was about to say. "What are you doing here? The gallery is closed."

Mikey blushed guiltily. "I ..." His shoulders slumped as he took a deep breath. "I couldn't stay away. I know I shouldn't be here, but I was getting cabin fever. I'm sorry, Mrs ..."

"Mikey, first, I thought we agreed you would call me Eve. Second, I understand how you feel. Believe me."

Mikey relaxed, and smiled at Eve. "There are always people at the door, checking to see if we're open yet. You being in the news again doesn't hurt." He quickly clamped his mouth shut.

Eve offered him a small smile. She didn't mind being in the news when it came to her work, but being the center of attention because of yet another murder? Once was enough for Eve. Any more than that, and it just got ridiculous. She was beginning to get tired of her problems herself.

"Well, let's not keep them waiting. I'm ready to open the gallery."

"Oh! Did they find the person doing all of this?"

"They're close." It wasn't necessarily a lie. For all she knew, they could have caught everyone involved. Billy hasn't been returning her incessant calls, and Eve was getting incredibly impatient. "It's still early. Let's open up."

"Eve."

Eve just stopped herself from flinching at Adam's angry voice. It certainly wouldn't do to let Mikey see her any way but in control.

Mikey, however, couldn't hide his discomfort. "Um … I think I'll just …" Mikey quickly walked out of the main room of the gallery.

Eve steeled herself, and turned to face an extremely pissed Adam.

"I thought we agreed you wouldn't come here until we knew it was safe."

"We did. But, I can't keep sitting around doing nothing, Adam."

"Not even with me asking you to do just that?"

Eve sighed, and gestured around her. "I need this, Adam. *This* is who I am. Stop trying to change me," she warned.

Surprise flashed across Adam's face. Did she really think he was trying to change her? "This is only part of who you are, Eve. You need to think about your family, too."

"I *am* thinking about you and Bella!" Eve snapped. "Bella isn't here with me, where I *want* her to be. You don't think that hurts me? But, I'm here because I'm trying to prevent being resentful towards *you*." Eve paced away. "I'm trying to prevent a lot of things," she finished quietly.

Adam stared after her, completely speechless by her admission. "You resent me?"

Eve walked back to him. "No. I resent whoever is doing this to me. I resent the fact that my gallery has, *once again*, been taken away from me. I resent not being able to paint because I don't feel inspired. I don't *want* to resent you." She cupped his face in her hands. "I love you, Adam. So incredibly much. And, as much as I love doing things for you, I don't want to be your secretary."

"I don't understand. When did I ever ask you to be my secretary?"

"You didn't, I'm sorry. It's just how I felt today looking for office space instead of being in my own office. Or, even my studio."

"You offered to look for space for me, Eve. If I knew it would make you feel ..."

"Stop. This isn't your fault. None of this is your fault." Eve lifted onto her toes, and brushed her lips softly against Adam's. "I need this, baby."

Damn it. How could he deny her when she says things like that? Adam studied Eve, weighing his options. He realized, looking at her, he had no other options except to give her what she needs. Besides, he made sure James had security on her at all times. He had to believe that was enough.

"Fine. But," he continued before she could say anything. "I would like you to call me or text me. Often. Can you do that without resenting me?"

Eve's brow raised. "I can do that," she answered evenly.

Adam's lips twitched. Just that one quirk of an eyebrow from her, and he was putty in her hands. He kissed her again, letting this one heat up just enough to leave her breathless when he pulled away.

"Thank you. I'll see you tonight, yeah?"

"Mmhmm." Holy hell, the man could kiss. Eve walked him to the elevator, mostly in hopes that she would get another kiss. "The warehouse," she said suddenly.

"Sorry?"

"My warehouse. It would be perfect for your firm." She noted his skeptical look, and smiled. "Hear me out. I know it's a little rough around the edges, but it has amazing potential. The light from the wall of windows is impeccable, and with your skills, I'm sure you can make it perfect."

"My skills, huh?" Adam's cocky grin made Eve laugh. "It sounds interesting. I'll go there and take a look around." He checked his watch. "However, since my attendance has been questionable today, it'll have to be tomorrow."

"Remind me to give you the keys tonight."

"Hmm." Adam stroked Eve's cheek with the pad of his thumb. "Be careful, please?"

"I'll be here all day, *amant*. Besides, the security detail you had James put on me will be around."

"He told you about that?"

"They aren't exactly discreet." She wrapped her arms around his waist. "Thank you. You didn't just think of me and Bella, but you thought of Lainey, too."

"Lainey is important to you, babe, and that makes her important to me. I'm actually surprised she's not here with you."

"I asked her not to come. I needed some time to myself," she answered Adam's curious look with a small shrug.

"Federal Bureau of Investigations, how may I direct your call?"

"Eve Riley for Agent William Donovan."

Eve waited on hold, tapping a pen on her desk. She was annoying the hell out of herself, but interestingly enough, it kept her from snapping at the operator when she came back on the line.

"I'm sorry, Agent Donovan is not available. May I take a message?"

"No, I've left enough messages. Thank you." Eve resisted the urge to pick up her phone and throw it across the room. This shit was disrupting her life, and she'd be damned if she let it go on any longer than it had to. She took out her cell and scrolled down to Billy's personal number.

Avoiding me is only pissing me off. Call me, or you will not like the consequences.

She pressed send, and sat back in her chair. Fortunately, Eve didn't have to wait long for a response this time, smiling sardonically when her phone rang.

"It's about time, Billy."

"You shouldn't threaten a federal agent, Eve," Billy chided.

"It wasn't a threat since you don't know what the consequences are." Eve rolled her shoulders, trying to release the tension she felt. "I asked you to work with Charlie and James, and you're shutting them out. By doing that, you're shutting me out. I don't appreciate that."

"I'm not shutting anyone out, Eve, I'm doing my job."

"I don't mind that you're doing your job, Billy. But, I need you to keep everyone else in the loop. If you can't do that, I don't want you on my case anymore."

Billy snickered, which only infuriated Eve more. "No matter how influential you are, you don't have the authority to take me off the case, Eve."

Eve took a deep breath, letting it out slowly as she counted to ten. "I can complain to your superiors about the job you're doing. Or, I can just tell you that if you don't do what I ask, you lose my friendship."

"Are you serious? You're threatening me with your friendship?"

"Yes. I will do anything to stop this threat against my family. I brought you in against the advice of others, Billy. But, make no mistake, your friendship is not worth the lives of my family."

Billy sucked in a breath. This is not how he envisioned this conversation going. He wanted to give Eve some good news. He wanted to let her know he had leads. But, he didn't, and she was pissed. Damn it.

"Eduardo Martinez," he told her.

"Excuse me?"

"The name of the alleged shooter is Eduardo Martinez. He didn't give us anything, and we didn't have enough to detain him..."

"You let him go?"

"We had no choice, Eve. We couldn't prove he was the shooter."

"If you had let James question him …"

"If James would have questioned him, nothing he would've gotten from him would've been admissible in court."

"I don't give a fuck about court! What I fucking care about is finding the damn person doing this to me! *This* is why I wanted James involved!" Eve pinched the bridge of her nose. Goddamnit why couldn't he have just listened to her? "You let the only person that could give us *any* information go!"

"We don't even know if he's the shooter, Eve."

"If James said he was the shooter, then he was!"

"Eve …"

"Fix it, Agent Donovan. Get him back."

"I am having him followed, and tracing his calls. If he is the shooter, maybe he'll call whomever he's working for."

"I hope he does. Keep the others informed." Eve hung up without a goodbye. She was too pissed off to offer him any pleasantries. If he let this guy go, and he was the shooter, Billy may have just helped whoever is putting her family in danger. She was about to dial Charlie when Mikey buzzed.

"Yes, Mikey?"

"Ms. Cummings is here to see you, ma'am."

Fantastic. "Send her up. How are things going down there?"

"Busy! But, I have it all under control," he said quickly.

Eve chuckled. "I'm sure you do. If you need any help, just let me know."

She would have to wait to call Charlie, instead she typed out a quick text.

Thinking of you.

She hesitated for a moment before hitting send, but was rewarded with an immediate response.

Thinking of you 2. Call me later?

Eve had just enough time to respond to Lainey with a yes before Dee knocked lightly on her door.

"Come in, Dee."

"There's certainly not a dull moment in your life, Mrs. Riley." Dee gave her a sly smile, sitting herself in the seat in front of Eve's desk, and crossing her legs.

"At least you waited until I came back to work to irritate me." Though she was only half teasing, she offered Dee an amicable smile. "How did you know I was here anyway?"

"I'm an investigative reporter, Eve. I know things, and if I don't know, I obtain someone who can find out for me."

Eve's eyes snapped to Dee's. "Eduardo Martinez."

Dee frowned. "The Brazilian hitman?"

Hitman? Billy didn't mention that bit of information. Either he was still keeping things from her, or he didn't know as much as Dee did. "You know him?"

"*Of* him. Thank God, I don't know him. Why are you interested in a hitman?"

"I'm not. Apparently, he's interested in me."

"No shit?" Dee's response was so out of character, both of Eve's brows raised in surprise. "That is not good, Eve. He's notorious in Brazil. Who the hell did you piss off there?"

"I don't know anyone in Brazil," Eve responded distractedly. She searched her memory for anyone that could be connected to her and Brazil, or even Tony. It's possible she doesn't know all of the people he owed, of course. "Do you know how to find him or contact him?"

"You want to contact the man who wants to kill you?"

"No. I'm not suicidal. I want to give James something to work with. If you have contact information, maybe he can work backwards and find out who hired this Mr. Martinez."

"You're taking a big risk, Eve."

"I think the bigger risk is sitting back and doing nothing while this guy is out there hunting me and my family."

Eve closed the door behind her, shutting out the black sedan that follows her. Annoying, she thought. At least when she had Adam and Lainey followed, she made sure they were discreet. But, after a call to Charlie and James about this apparent hitman, she supposed security being visible to everyone wasn't such a bad idea.

"Eve?"

"Yeah, baby, I'm here," she called. After a heavy sigh, she squared her shoulders, and went to find Adam to tell him about her day. Shit. She was not looking forward to this.

"A hitman."

Eve took a bite of her stuffed Portobello mushroom, and nodded nonchalantly. Bella was banging her sippy cup on her highchair tray, talking about what was obviously extremely important baby things. Eve gave Bella a smile, and a small piece of mushroom.

"A hitman, Eve?"

Adam had been stunned like this ever since Eve told him the story. She couldn't blame him.

"Yes, *amant*, that's what Dee said. Charlie and James are on it, and doing everything they can to find who hired him."

"How can you be so blasé about this?"

"I'm not, baby. But, I refuse to let this take over my life, especially here at home."

"I get that, beautiful, but we still need to be on alert. Even here."

"We are. James put more security around the house, we have a state of the art alarm system, and just because I'm calm, that doesn't mean I'm not careful."

Adam nodded, and tried being calm himself. "And, you don't know anyone in Brazil?"

"As I told Charlie, I've only been to Brazil once, and I doubt my dealings there left anyone wanting to kill me. I bought art there for a lot of money, then left."

"Tony?" Fuck, he hated saying his name, especially to Eve.

"I can't be sure, but I'm hoping James will have better luck on that end." Eve caught Bella's sippy cup as she chunked it at her. "Momma doesn't want to talk about this anymore either, baby girl. How about you, me and daddy go play before bath time?"

Adam smiled at both of them. If she wants to give Bella normalcy, he would give it to her. But, he would be calling James and getting a full report.

Eve lay on the bed, her legs bent and crossed at the knee. She tapped her toe to an imaginary beat as she waited for Lainey to answer her call.

"Hey, there. How was the gallery?"

"Busy. Seems having drama in my life really boosts patrons."

"You know, I can come in and help tomorrow," Lainey said hopefully. She missed Eve, of course, but she also missed the gallery as much as Eve did.

"I really don't think Jack will approve after I tell you about my day."

Lainey was eerily quiet while Eve told her everything, only emitting a small gasp when she heard the word hitman.

"Where is Adam?" Lainey asked softly when Eve was finished.

"On a call to James." Eve was pretty sure Adam didn't think she knew what he was up to, but she did. And, she was fine with it if it gave him any sense of control or safety.

"He's still letting you go to the gallery?"

Eve balked at the word 'letting'. It was petty, she knew, but she didn't like feeling as though she needed permission.

"I have security, Lainey," she said coolly.

"Eve, honey, don't get upset with me. I didn't mean it the way it sounded. This is a lot to process ..." Lainey picked up a jade statue of Buddha with rubies and diamonds encrusted in the necklace around the neck, and held it close. The portly little fella had been a gift from Eve. A sixty-thousand dollar gift that sometimes made Lainey afraid to even touch it, but she loved it nonetheless. "I'm going to the gallery with you, tomorrow. Jack knows there's still a risk. He doesn't need the details."

"Are you sure that's a good idea?"

"No. Now ask me if I care. I want to be near you, Eve. Please?"

A slight pang filled Eve's heart. Lainey was afraid. Afraid of being with Eve, but also afraid of not being there and losing Eve. "Alright. You should know, though, we are surrounded by security. Everything will be okay."

∞

Eve glanced up from her iPad to see Adam watching her. The memory of the night before flooded her mind just then as she saw the raw emotion in his eyes. There was no hurry last night, no demands, just pure love and devotion. He took his time with her, kissing every inch of her until it built a need so fierce in both of them, it was impossible to stay apart. Even when he took her, he did it slow—almost painfully so—building up her orgasm to the highest peak, she had nowhere else to go but come crashing down in a powerful euphoria.

She leaned over and kissed Adam chastely. "I'll be okay, baby. I won't leave the gallery until I'm ready to come home. I promise."

Eve couldn't forget the threat against Adam, the knife lodged in the portrait she had painted. While he was worried about her, she was more worried for him. But, she couldn't keep him from his job. He had worked way too hard to get this prestigious account, so she had to trust in the men James had watching over Adam.

"Promise me you will be careful," she demanded.

"I promise, beautiful. I won't let anyone take me away from you or Bella." He kissed her forehead, her eyelids, her cheeks, her chin, as though his lips were memorizing everything about the way she felt beneath them. "I'll be at the site today, near the warehouse. I'll go over and take a look during lunch."

Eve frowned. "Are you sure that's a good idea?"

Well, this was an odd turn. Now she was worried about him going out. What a pair they made.

"I have security, too. Plus, I want to get the new offices going soon while I'm still being recognized for the Griffen account. I'll be quick. I just want to check out the layout, take a few pictures, and get an idea."

Eve stood and walked to the small built-in desk area of the kitchen. Opening a drawer, she shuffled a few things around before finding the key. She took it back to him, held it out, then snatched it back before he could take it.

"Be careful."

"I promise."

Eve stood with Adam at the front door and kissed him deeply. She didn't care that guys in dark sedans were watching them, or the neighbor watering her plants looked on in shock. She wanted him to know how much she love him, and poured every ounce of that love into the kiss.

"I'm so in love with you, baby," she whispered.

Adam pressed his forehead to hers, his hand on the back of her head to hold her there. "And, I'm so in love with you, beautiful. I'll see you tonight, yeah?"

"Yes. Maybe I'll make pork tonight. Sound good?" It was her attempt at normalcy, and he smiled.

"Perfect." Adam gave her another quick kiss before turning towards the car. "Good morning, Lainey."

Lainey grinned at him, having seen the Eve and Adam kissing show herself. For once, she wasn't jealous. Well, not completely anyway. She stood by Eve, watching her watch Adam, winking that sexy wink, and waving until he disappeared. When Eve's smile faded, Lainey became concerned.

"Eve? What's wrong?"

Eve shivered next to Lainey, and crossed her arms to rub her hands over them. The beautiful spring day had nothing to do with the chills, but, still, she looked at Lainey and smiled. "Nothing. Want some coffee?"

They sat silently for a time, watching Lexie with Bella, just enjoying the moment. Bella's beautiful laugh made Eve smile and tear up at the same time. Eve's baby girl was everything to her, and the thought of something happening ...

"Lexie, could you take Bella into the other room, please?"

Lexie looked up in surprise. Eve usually loved this time of the morning with Bella, but something seemed off today. "Yes, ma'am, of course."

Eve held her sigh in at the 'ma'am', taking Bella's chubby cheeks in her hand. "Momma loves you, baby girl." She kissed her loudly, making Bella laugh. "I'll be in to say goodbye before I have to leave," she told Lexie, then waited until they were gone.

"Why do I feel like I'm not going to like whatever you have to say?" Lainey sat back in her chair, and put her hands on her hips. "Don't give me that sexy eyebrow thing, I know you. You're about to piss me off, aren't you?"

"There's just something I want to talk to you about. I should have done it a while ago, but ... well, this stuff that's going on made me think I should do it now."

Lainey looked at Eve wearily. "I'm really not going to like this."

Eve took a breath. No, Lainey wasn't going to like what she had to ask, but it needed to be asked. "Lainey, honey, if something happens to me ..."

"No! No, no, no, no. Nothing is going to happen to you, so just stop right there!"

"Lainey, please. I'm not just talking about now. If anything, no matter when it is, happens to me and A ..." Eve stumbled on Adam's name, not even wanting to think of that possibility. She cleared her throat and tried again. "If something happens to us, I need to know you will take care of Bella."

Flawed Perfection

Lainey didn't want to think about this, especially now. But, one look at Eve told her Eve needed this peace of mind. "Of course I would! I love Bella, Eve. But, nothing is going to happen to either of you!"

Eve just smiled, and continued. "If something happens to me, help Adam? Be there for him?"

"Eve, you have to stop this, please."

"I will, Lainey, as soon as I know ..."

"Yes! I will be there for Adam." Good Lord, she hoped Eve was done, because she didn't know how much more of this she could take without bursting into tears.

But, Eve wasn't done.

"And, if something happened to ... if ..." Eve couldn't finish. She couldn't imagine a life without Adam, not now. Just the mere thought had her trembling, and her eyes watering.

Lainey laid a hand on Eve's and squeezed gently. "I'll be there for you," she said quietly.

Eve nodded and sniffed. "If something happened to him because of me, I don't know if I could live with that." Eve shook herself mentally, and heard Bella's laughter from the other room. "Don't let her forget about me."

"Eve, baby, Bella is going to have you around for a very long time. You're going to teach her wonderful things, annoy her when she becomes a teenager, and see her grow into a beautiful woman, just like her mom." Lainey felt Eve's hand grasp on to hers, and swallowed the lump in her throat. "I will never let her forget you, honey."

"The locket that my mom gave me is in the top drawer of my desk at the gallery. It belongs to Bella. Give it to her?"

"Okay, that's enough. Eve, I can't listen to you talk like this anymore. You're scaring the hell out of me, not to mention depressing me." Lainey stood up and walked to the window overlooking the backyard. "I will do what you ask, Eve, because I love Bella and I care very much for Adam. But, did you ever think about how *I* would cope without you?"

Eve's heart ached. Yes, she thought of that, quite a bit. She just didn't know what to offer Lainey as comfort. She went to Lainey, touching her lightly, and leaning her body in to hers.

"*I love you. I will always be with you no matter where I am.*"

Lainey trembled as a tear slid down her cheek. She knew it was all Eve could offer her, but to Lainey, it was everything.

Chapter Fourteen

Eve had been on edge all day. The gallery was full of people, but she left them in Lainey and Mikey's capable hands, and retreated to her office. She tried sketching, hoping it would help, only there were more pieces of wadded up paper on the floor than sketches in front of her.

She called Dee, who told her that all the information she came up with she passed to Charlie and James. Eve called Charlie, who told her nothing solid has come up, yet, but he's working closely with James. She even called Billy to see if his traces produced anything. They didn't. Son of a bitch, she was becoming one of *those* people. Those annoying, calling constantly for updates, 'are-we-there-yet' people. But, she couldn't help it. If she could just find one piece of this damn puzzle, it would give her something to go on. When Tony was after her, at least she knew her opponent. However, now Eve was completely in the dark, and grasping at straws did nothing to help calm her down.

She hated this feeling. Sickness sat in the pit of her stomach, churning into a fear she couldn't tame. Even years ago, when she was being brutalized, she'd had a plan. She had survived because she knew she would get out. Eve couldn't guarantee that she would get out of this one. Nor could she guarantee the safety of those she held so dear. It was a humbling and terrifying feeling.

Unable to sit and basically twiddle her thumbs, Eve got up to pace. She found her feet taking her to the balcony overlooking her gallery. It was clean now, all reminisces of the vandalism were gone with fresh paint and restored art. Everything looked … normal. She could stand here and pretend that everything was normal, if it weren't for uneasiness she felt inside.

She watched Mikey push his glasses up, and smile genuinely at a customer. He would make the sale, she knew. Being so personable always worked in his favor. Her gaze switched to Lainey, who was also with a customer—a full gallery was the silver lining of all of the drama. Eve knew Lainey would also make a sale, or three. She was charming and witty, and extremely intelligent about the art she spoke of. Of course, being beautiful didn't hurt with the male—and some female—customers.

Lainey felt a tingle down her spine, and turned to look up. Her eyes locked with Eve's. She tried to identify all of the emotions she saw flicker across Eve's features, but was pulled back into the conversation with her customer. When she got the chance to look again, Eve had disappeared.

∞

Eve sat at her desk, pen poised. Maybe it was morbid to do what she was doing, but better safe than sorry. Isn't that what they say? She turned off the chatter in her mind, and wrote from her heart.

Flawed Perfection

Adam, my love,

When you first came into my life, I wasn't in the best frame of mind. I told myself over and over again that I didn't want a relationship. But, one look at you, one touch of your hand, or brush of your lips, and there was no way I could stay away. You enchanted me from the very beginning, and I should have known then that I wouldn't be able to keep my heart out of it. The first time you kissed me, I fell in love with you. Of course, I denied it, and you, out of fear, but I know now that what I felt for you was pure. I never knew what it was like to be kissed and made love to until I met you. You opened my eyes to so many things, and for that I will always be grateful. I'm sorry it took me so long to let you in, but I can't tell you how happy you made me by waiting for me. You've given me your love, your devotion, your everything, and best of all, you gave me Bella. The gift of our baby girl is like giving me back a part of my soul that I lost when I lost my mom. I will never be able to thank you enough for that. You are my love, my life, and I am completely honored and blessed that you chose to be with me. If you are reading this letter, my love, it means I can no longer be with you or our daughter. I'm sorry I had to leave you, but I will be with you always. I am so in love with you, baby, and I will be for eternity. Take care of yourself, and our baby girl. Tell her how much I love her every day. And, every day, remember how much I love you. Forever and always yours.

Love, Eve

Damn. When she made the decision to write these letters, she didn't consider how incredibly hard it would be. Eve knew that the next letter would be even more difficult. She drew in a deep breath, and began writing.

My Dearest Bella,

My baby girl. I wish so much that I could be there with you to see you grow into a beautiful woman. Always know that I am here, watching over you. I am proud of you. No matter what you choose to do with your life, I support you as long as you're happy and healthy. I will give you what my mother gave me.

Flawed Perfection

I give you my strength to triumph through times of adversity and become the woman I know you were meant to be. I give you the courage to walk away from those who hurt you, with your head held high. I give you my heart, full of love, to add to yours so that you can pass it on to the world.

I know you will conquer this world, baby girl, but do it with kindness and dignity. Be generous in heart and soul, and I promise you, you will find happiness. Let yourself love and be loved, because it will be the one thing in life that brings you the most joy. I know that love exists, baby girl, because of your daddy. Find a man like him, and you will have everything you will ever need or want.

I love you, my sweet Bella, and I am there with you, always.

Love,

Mom

∞

A single tear drop fell on the page before Eve folded it, and stuffed it into and envelope and writing Bella's name on the front. Then, she took out one more piece of paper, and stared at it for a moment, before beginning to write.

Dear Lainey,

What can I say to you that could ever convey the gratitude I have for you? Your friendship came at a time when I desperately needed it. I thought that the only way to keep from getting hurt was to close myself off to anyone and everyone. You showed me how much I was missing, and you did it by loving me for who I was on the inside. You know as well as I do that people tend to only see what they want to see when they look at a beautiful painting. Take Dali, for instance. Your favorite. Someone may look at a Dali and see the picture as a whole. But, you? You see every detail that went in to developing that art. Every nuance, every hidden feature. You did the same with me. No matter how much I tried to keep it from you, you broke through, and saw me.

It's because of you that I have a family. It's because of you that the art that adorns my home now comes from my *daughter. And it's because of you that I was able to allow Adam into my heart. Grateful doesn't even begin to describe how I feel about that.*

Never forget, though, my love for you. You are the best friend I've ever had, and so much more. I cherish our moments together, and I always will. You and your boys were the first of my family. Spending time with the three of you meant the world to me. It made me realize that I had more of myself to offer.

If you're reading this, then I hope you're keeping your promise and taking care of Bella and Adam. Watch over my baby girl, Lainey. Guide her the way you think I would guide her. And, tell them daily that I love them. No matter where I am, I love them. Be happy, Lainey. I'm always with you.

Love,

Eve

―――∞―――

Shit. That was enough of that. For once, Eve was glad she didn't have a wealth of family. Any more letters like that and she'd be a basket case. Because he was on her mind, she took her phone out to text Adam.

Hey baby. Day going well?

She knew he would think she was checking up on him, and maybe she was. But, she also just wanted some connection with him. Since he told her he would be at the site today, she didn't think calling him would be wise. Eve grinned when her phone chimed.

Never as good as when I hear from you.

Eve's grin widened at his response. It felt nice to smile after being so depressed by the letters she wrote.

Such a charmer ;)

Absently, Eve picked up the pencil she had tossed aside when frustration made her stop trying to sketch.

Not a charmer, beautiful. Honest. Checking in on me?

Hmm. Definitely a charmer, Eve thought. She lifted her wrist to check the time, then remembered she didn't wear a watch. Why did she always do that? She switched her gaze to her phone and noted it was past lunch time. Adam should have been to the warehouse by now.

Just wondering if you checked out the space? I still think it's perfect.

Eve began sketching, distractedly, thinking of the warehouse. She didn't know why she hadn't thought of it before. Of course, she had a lot of shit on her mind.

Not yet, beautiful. Had to work through lunch. Will do it on the way out. Is that OK?

Eve smiled again. She was still getting used to this whole marriage thing. He didn't have to ask her for permission, but the fact that he did warmed her heart.

Of course, amant. Be careful. Bella and I will be waiting patiently for you. Or, maybe impatiently on my part. ;)

She went back to her sketch as she waited for his response. Nothing good was coming out of it, she thought. It bothered her, greatly, that she couldn't paint or sketch. This was the first time in her life that she couldn't find the inspiration. She wasn't completely sure how to deal with that. Maybe she would get in the studio tonight and stay there until something broke through.

I'll make it worth your wait, beautiful. I promise. ;) I won't be long.

Or, she would just take Adam out to the studio and stay there until he fucked the inspiration out of her.

Chapter Fifteen

"Eve?" Lainey glanced over at Eve for what seemed to be the hundredth time since leaving the gallery. She had been so quiet and despondent, so unlike Eve, that Lainey worried.

"Hmm?"

"Is everything okay?"

Eve looked at Lainey briefly and offered her a small smile. "Of course." *As okay as it can be when, once again, your life is being threatened.*

Lainey bit back her sigh. She hated when Eve was like this with her. If she didn't want to talk to her, she should say so, not lie. "Why can't you just talk to me?" she thought, staring out the window.

Eve frowned. "What would you like me to say, Lainey?"

Lainey flinched. Had she really said that out loud? Well, since she had, she may as well see it through.

"I don't want you to say everything is okay when clearly it's not."

Eve slowed her Jag, turning into a parking lot. She noted that the dark sedan followed her, parking a not-so-respectable fifty feet away. *Ugh. Boundaries, guys.* She pushed them aside, and turned in her seat to face Lainey.

"I'm scared. Is that what you want to hear?" She watched Lainey's features soften and fought back tears. "I don't know what to do, or how to deal with this. I don't know what to do to keep my family safe. Hell, I don't know if, when I walk out the door, I will come back."

"Eve …"

"Don't. Please. I didn't want to say anything because I don't want you to worry more than I already know you are. And, I didn't want to say anything because this feeling of weakness pisses me off."

"Being scared doesn't make you weak, Eve." Lainey told her softly.

"If I just knew what I was up against …"

"You have people working on that for you, Eve. Let them do their jobs."

"That's what I'm doing, Lainey." Eve looked over her shoulder at the security. "But, this is not what I'm used to." She turned back to Lainey. "I'm sorry."

"For what?" Eve's apology surprised her. What did she possibly have to be sorry about? She didn't do this.

"I'm sorry that being in my life has put yours in danger. Again."

"Eve, don't you dare do that. This is not your fault. Tony wasn't your fault. People make their own choices." She glanced over at the sedan herself before taking Eve's hand in hers. "I made my own choices, and I wouldn't change a thing."

Eve gently squeezed Lainey's hand and smiled. "You're sweet. And, I'm just tired and frustrated. I'll feel much better when Charlie and James find something."

Lainey slipped her hand away. Not that she didn't want to keep holding Eve's hand, but lately she had been remembering why she made the decision to stay with Jack. She also remembered why Eve chose Adam, especially after that spectacular kiss this morning. "I notice you didn't mention Billy."

Eve snickered and pulled back onto the road. She was ready to get home to her daughter and wait for Adam. "It's petty, I know, but he kept things from me, so this is my way of punishing him."

"So you're keeping him out of the loop now?"

"He's working his own angle, as the feds usually do. He'll text me every once in a while with absolutely no updates. I'll call him sometimes with the same results. It just gets a little uncomfortable talking to him knowing he still harbors these feelings for me."

Lainey stiffened, and Eve felt the change, immediately regretting what she said.

"I didn't mean you, Lainey. You know our situation is different. I have never had feelings for Billy."

"May I ask why?"

Eve looked at Lainey questioningly.

"Billy is a good-looking guy and sweet. He obviously thinks the world of you."

"It took me a long time to open up to a man like Adam. Do you really think I had the capacity to have feelings for Billy at that time of my life?"

"That makes sense."

Eve placed the pork in the oven with the potatoes, and set the timer. She would work on the salad when she knew Adam was on his way home. She chose a good vintage, red wine and popped it open to let it breathe. Once she finished that, she turned her attention to Bella—who kept bumping into her with her activity walker—and plucked her up.

"Is momma not giving you enough attention, baby girl?"

Bella made Eve's heart swell with love by giving her a string of 'mama, mama, mama's' while patting Eve's cheeks.

"*I love you so much.*" Eve whispered to her, hugging her almost too tightly. "Let's text daddy and see where he is."

She sat at the table, balancing Bella on her lap. Bringing out her phone, she typed out a quick text.

Hey baby. Do you have an ETA?

Bella reached for Eve's phone, swiping her fingers across the screen, laughing when the icons moved. Eve chuckled at her daughter, and placed a kiss on top of her head. When it chimed, Bella squealed with laughter.

No. Shouldn't be long though.

Eve frowned. He must be in a bad mood. Adam never texted her back without some sort of endearment.

Everything OK?

Bella fidgeted in Eve's arms, so she let her down to tool around.

Fine. Just trying to finish up.

Okay, Eve did not enjoy cranky Adam's texts. And, she couldn't shake the feeling that something more was wrong. Why she decided to ask the question, she didn't know, but she typed it out with trembling fingers.

OK. Is chicken still perfect for dinner?

Please, she prayed silently. Please give the right answer.

Yes. It's fine.

Fuck! She scrolled to Adam's number and called. Her breathing and heartbeat came faster, and she took a breath to try and calm herself. Maybe he just forgot she was making pork. It's been a stressful time for both of them, it would be perfectly understandable.

When the line answered, she waited for his greeting, but heard nothing.

"Who is this?" she demanded.

Silence.

"Who is this? Where is my husband!" Unable to sit, Eve shoved out of the chair and began pacing. "Tell me!" She practically screamed in the phone, and Bella began to cry.

The line went dead, and Eve almost screamed again out of frustration and fear. She was about to dial Adam's number again when the phone chimed in her hand making her jump.

Don't call again, Eve. If you want to see your husband again, you'll wait for my instructions. Call anyone else, and he dies.

Oh God. Oh no. Please, no. Eve's entire body shuddered with uncontrollable shakes. She sank to her knees next to Bella, who was still crying after Eve's outburst. Eve took Bella into her arms, holding on for dear life.

"I'm sorry, baby girl. It was supposed to be me, not your daddy." Eve began to cry with Bella, rocking them both. *God, please, let me help him. Let me save him. I can't live without him. He's done nothing to deserve this except love me. Please, let him be okay.* Eve kept repeating the silent prayer over and over, wishing the phone would signal with instructions. She would do anything to save him. She would lay down her life for him if she had to.

She picked up her phone, incapable of waiting. She just hoped she didn't make things worse.

Please. Tell me what you want. I will do anything.

She could barely hold the phone in her trembling hands, and waiting for any kind of response was killing her. Her heart pounded in her chest, so hard she was sure it would break through. Her only source of solace was Bella. She had settled down, but even her one year old self focused on Eve as though she knew something was wrong.

I want you to lose everything. You're going to watch as those you love are taken away from you.

Bile rose in Eve's throat, and she swallowed multiple times to keep it down.

Who are you? What did I do to you? I'm begging you, please let my husband go. Take me.

Think Eve. Think, think, think. Who could hate you this much? She couldn't imagine anyone other than Tony, and he was dead.

Tempting offer. Come say goodbye, Eve. Be here at 9pm, and make sure no one follows you. If I see anyone with you, he dies.

The text included an address that wasn't familiar to Eve. She sat there staring at the text. It could only have been a few seconds, but it felt like an eternity before she was able to move. *Come say goodbye, Eve.*

No. She would find a way out of this. At least for Adam. She would be damned if she let anything happen to him because of someone's hatred for her.

Chapter Sixteen

Her mind was reeling. If she wanted to do something for Adam, she was going to have to calm herself down and think. Easier said than done, she thought bitterly as she fought nausea, tears and a complete and utter break down.

Do it for Adam! Eve's inner scolding helped a little, and she found herself wondering where the hell Adam's security had been. How was he taken? Damn it. If something had happened to them as well, that was just more for Eve to take responsibility for. Her body count was rising.

Bella tugged on Eve's pant leg, and looking down at her daughter, Eve knew exactly what she needed to do. She checked the time on the phone. She had a little more than an hour to get everything she needed to do done.

Eve stooped to pick Bella up, and took her to the desk in the kitchen. She gave Bella a piece of paper and a crayon, sitting her on the floor next to her. Grabbing a piece of paper herself, she scribbled precise instructions. Eve read over it, and when she was satisfied, she stuffed it in an envelope, snapped up the three letters she wrote earlier, and picked Bella up. Bella grasped on to her mom's shirt collar, keeping her crayon with her, as Eve raced upstairs.

Eve threw Bella's diaper bag onto the changing table, and started packing clothes for her. She couldn't make it obvious, so the packing had to be light. Anything else that was needed could be bought. She slipped the letters in the side pocket, and zipped it closed.

Eve took out her phone, scrolled down to the name she needed, and made the call. Once that was done, she once again found the name she needed, pressed it and waited with fear struggling to take her over.

"Eve? Hey."

"Hi, Lainey. I need you to do me a favor."

"Of course."

"In five minutes, I need you to meet me outside and tell me that you're glad I could come over and keep you company since Jack has to leave."

There was silence on the other end.

"Lainey! Please, can you do this for me?"

"Eve, what's going on?"

"I will explain what I can when I get there, just please. Five minutes. Make sure you're loud enough for the security guys to hear you."

"Okay," Lainey responded tentatively.

Eve ended the call, and situated Bella and her diaper bag. Trekking back downstairs, Eve slipped on her sneakers. She was glad now that she had changed into jeans and a t-shirt when she got home. Not knowing what she was up against, any bit of comfort was welcome. She checked the phone again. It was time. Squaring her shoulders, she took a breath, plastered on a smile and walked out the front door.

Her heart was hammering in her chest. This had to work, or Adam could die. When she saw Lainey walking towards her, she ramped up her smile, hoping Lainey would follow suit. Eve sent up a silent prayer of thank you when she did.

"Hey!" Lainey called. "Thank you so much for keeping me company. I didn't want to be alone while Jack had to go out."

Lainey took the diaper bag from Eve, and even though the questions were in her eyes, she kept her smile and easiness. Eve wouldn't be able to thank her enough.

"Not a problem. It's my pleasure."

They walked to Lainey's front door together, two women, carefree and happy. That's how they would look to the eyes watching them. Once inside, Eve's façade faltered. She could stand there and crumble, or she could do what she needed to do.

Lainey closed them in, immediately turning to Eve.

"What is going on?"

"They have Adam." Eve's voice trembled saying it out loud. Focus! You said it, now you have to fix it!

"Oh my God! Did you call Charlie?"

"No!" Eve winced at the harshness of her voice, and took a steady—or a steady as she could get—breath. "I can't call anyone. If they see me with anyone, they'll …" her voice hitched. Eve couldn't bring herself to say the words, so she left it hanging.

"What do you mean if they see you? Eve, you can't go after them by yourself!"

"I don't have a choice, Lainey."

"You'll get killed!"

"If I don't go, they'll ki ... goddammit!" One more not-so-steady breath. "They want me to lose everything."

"Who!"

"I don't know! God, I wish I knew." Eve crushed Bella to her, hugging her fiercely. *"Momma loves you, baby girl,"* she whispered before handing her to Lainey. "Take her."

"Eve ..."

"Lainey? What's ... Oh, Eve, I didn't know you were here." Jack looked from Eve to Lainey to Bella and back again. The fear in the room was almost palpable. "What's going on?"

"Jack," Eve tried to hold back the desperation in her voice, but didn't succeed. "You have to get the boys, take them and Lainey, and ... Bella out of here."

"I don't understand."

"They have Adam. They're threatening everyone I hold dear. Please, I don't have much time."

Jack instantly went after the boys, calling them to pack get dressed.

Eve took the instructions out of the diaper bag, and handed them over to Lainey. "You're going to get on my plane. Steve is picking the destination. I won't know."

"Eve, there has to be another way."

"There isn't. Once you're on the plane, wait ten minutes, then open this and follow the instructions. Ten minutes, Lainey. Do not do it before. I need to know you understand this. I need to keep Bella, and you, safe. In order to do that, you have to do exactly what I ask."

Lainey nodded, unable to speak over the lump that formed in her throat.

"I'm going to borrow Jack's truck. It's the only one they're not following."

Lainey nodded again.

"Give me a five minute head start, then load everyone up and get to the plane. Once you're in the hangar, there will be people there to hold off security. Steve is instructed to take off as soon as you get there. Are you clear so far?"

"*Yes.*"

"There are a few clothes for Bella, but Steve will give you the money you need to buy other things. Clothes, necessities and anything else."

"We can take care of that."

"I don't have time to argue with you, honey. Just do as I ask."

Lainey nodded, again. Her entire body seemed to shake uncontrollably, and she clutched Bella tighter to her.

Eve saw the movement, and tears sprang to her eyes. Lainey would keep her safe. She moved closer, taking Bella's face in her palms. "I love you." She kissed Bella gently on the cheek, then glanced over Lainey's shoulders. Jack and the boys were still getting things ready. Eve hugged both Lainey and Bella to her, holding on as though it was the last time she would see them. God, she hoped it wasn't. "*I love you, both.*" She whispered, kissing Lainey's cheek. "Take care of her."

"You take care of yourself, Eve."

"I have to go. Explain everything to Jack. Explain that the instructions need to be followed or something will happen to Adam."

"I will. Jack's keys are by the garage door."

Eve nodded. When she made a move to leave, Lainey grasped her arm. "Come back. Both of you. Please, Eve, I'm begging you."

"I'll do my best, Lainey.

Chapter Seventeen

Eve pulled her hair into a messy bun, and borrowed one of Jack's caps to pull over her head. *Please work.* The mantra kept repeating in her head, over and over, as the garage door lifted and she carefully backed out Jack's Ford F150. The windows were tinted enough where she thought she had a chance to get past the sedans without being noticed. *Please work.*

When she turned off her street, she checked the rearview mirror constantly to see if she was being followed. It was only when she made it to the expressway without a sign of anyone trailing her, that she gunned it. Traffic was surprisingly light, and, again, she sent up a silent prayer. She had a little more than thirty minutes to get to her destination, and according to the GPS, she was only twenty minutes away.

Eve tried coming up with a plan, but there was nothing for her to go on. With Bella and Lainey, she knew what she needed to do. Just get them out of here. With Adam, she had no idea what or who she was up against, so trying to plan anything was a waste of time. She could only do what she was told. She would walk into this blindly, and then do everything she possibly could to keep Adam alive. She could only hope that Lainey would follow her instructions exactly.

When the building she was ordered to come to came into view, Eve killed the lights on Jack's truck and pulled in. The tires crunched over the rocks and dirt, making it that more ominous to Eve. With ten minutes to spare, Eve cut the engine and took in her surroundings with the help of street lamps.

It was an old, dilapidated warehouse, encompassed by a chain link fence topped with rusted barbed-wire. Behind the building, the river. Whomever was fucking with her, just led her into a trap. There was nowhere for Adam and her to go if they got out, except the way she goes in. She left the key in the ignition, the doors unlocked and the windows down.

Eve tucked her phone into her pocket, took off the cap she had borrowed from Jack, drew in a breath and stepped out of the truck. She listened carefully to every sound, not knowing how many people she would be up against. She heard nothing but the faint noise of distant traffic and honking horns. It did nothing to help her confidence that someone would be around to help. Checking the phone once more for the time, she carefully pushed through the rusted door, hating how it creaked to announce her arrival.

She stood just inside the door, her eyes trying to adjust to darkness. It was eerily quiet, but she could feel Adam's presence. It killed every bit of hope she had that this was just a ploy to get her alone.

"I'm here," she called, her voice echoing back to her. When she wasn't acknowledged, she tried again. "I'm here! I'm alone! I did what you asked, now where is my husband?!"

The bright light blinded her, and Eve raised a hand to shield her eyes. Once they adjusted, she squinted around her and saw him.

"Oh God! Adam!"

He was strapped to a chair, his beautiful face bloodied. All she wanted to do was get to him, but when her legs started moving Adam cried out in pain. Eve stopped abruptly. "Stop! Please, don't hurt him!"

Eve's phone chimed, and she scolded herself for not turning off the sound. She was so afraid that the sound would lead to Adam getting hurt again, that she considered throwing the phone across the room.

"He wants you to check the phone, baby."

Adam's voice sounded so small and filled with pain it made Eve flinch. She almost didn't comprehend what he said until the phone chimed again. Quickly, she took the phone out and checked the text.

Don't come near him. What I want from you now is for you to tell him the truth.

Eve frowned. Adam knew everything about her. What was she supposed to say?

"I don't understand. What do you want me to say?" Eve called out again.

Adam gritted his teeth as the pain seared through him. He tried so hard to hold in the agonizing sound that wanted to escape for Eve's sake. Unfortunately, he was too weak and the howl ripped through him.

"Please! Stop! I'm begging you. I will tell him whatever you want. Just tell me what to say!" Eve's voice came out as a sobbing plea, but seeing Adam in pain drained her of courage.

Adam closed his eyes. Seeing Eve like this was destroying him. He didn't know who the person doing this to her was, but Adam wanted nothing more than to kill him. He could also figure out what he wanted Eve to tell him. It was the only secret she hasn't revealed to him.

"He wants you to tell me about your affair with Lainey, Eve."

Eve's eyes widened in complete and utter shock. "*What?*" She stared at Adam with a mix of fear and guilt. She couldn't find the strength to respond, or tear her eyes away from him. Eve's phone chimed, making her jump. Her hands shook like an earthquake as she checked the text.

You told him?

Eve shook her head in a daze.

Then he speculates. Tell him. Everything.

Eve forced her eyes back to Adam. He was watching her closely, but she couldn't see any anger or hatred in him. Maybe he was too hurt physically. Of course she had hurt him emotionally. How could she forgive herself for that? How could he forgive her?

She couldn't find words. What does she say? If she took too much time, would he be tortured again? Because of her.

"You knew?" She finally asked carefully.

Adam's throat constricted. He hadn't been completely sure until just then. He couldn't deny that it hurt. A lot. With the added pressure, his dry throat burned.

"Of course I knew," he rasped, and tried clearing his throat. "You never let anyone in, Eve. I knew Lainey was different when you took her away and let her stay with you."

Eve stood there, unable to move from the shock. She stared at Adam. Why she didn't find betrayal behind those swollen eyes, she couldn't fathom. Her legs buckled beneath her and she dropped.

"I'm sorry. I'm so sorry, Adam." Tears didn't come, but she hoped he could hear how heartfelt the apology was.

"Has it happened since we've been married?" God, he didn't want to ask that question, but he couldn't stop himself.

"No! No, baby, it hasn't."

His heart lightened a tiny bit at her answer, but there was more he needed to know.

"Have you wanted it to?" Adam watched as she lowered her head in shame, and he knew. But, he needed to hear her say it. "The truth, Eve."

"*Yes.*"

Fuck that hurt. So, why didn't he hate her? Why wasn't he pissed at her?

"Why didn't you?"

She looked up at him in shock. "Because of you!"

"Do you love her?"

"Of course I do," she answered honestly.

"Are you in love with her?"

"I'm in love with you, Adam."

"Eve. Answer me."

"Adam, I love Lainey. She's my best friend. She helped me open my heart. Once I was able to do that, you were there. *You* are my heart. I'm *in love* with *you*." Eve placed her hand over her heart. "Forgive me, baby. Please."

Adam was silent for a moment. He studied the woman he loved, on her knees in front of him, asking him to forgive her. Eve Sumptor. A woman who had been to hell and back, more than once in her life. Lainey helped her. He should be grateful, right? He was jealous as hell, but could he understand?

Eve held her breath as she watched him process everything. The person doing this must be waiting for his answer just as much as Eve. If she didn't see Adam's wounds, or see him bound to the chair, and been forced to stay more than thirty feet away from him, she would've forgotten where they were and what was happening.

"I forgive you," he said finally, his voice just barely above a whisper.

Eve's breath left her in a rush, and she dropped her hands to the floor, sucking in another breath. She saw the uncertainty, but she would prove to him that he made the right choice. Just as she did.

"No!" The outburst of anger startled both Eve and Adam. "You are not supposed to forgive the bitch!"

Oh God! That voice! She knows that voice. Heard it in her nightmares for years before Adam chased them away.

"*Laurence.*"

Chapter Eighteen

Eve stood on shaky legs. She refused to be on her knees in front of him again.

"Why? Why are you doing this to me?"

"You took everything that was precious away from me, Eve."

His French accent saying her name made her skin crawl. To other women, this man would be considered handsome with his blonde hair, cropped close in a sophisticated cut, and sprinkled with just a touch of salt and pepper. His eyes, although cold and evil to Eve, were a warm golden brown. She had wished for years that she didn't know that. His body was long and lean, strong, especially when raping a seventeen year old girl ...

Eve swallowed hard to keep from getting sick. There was nothing handsome or good about this man. She knew him for exactly what he was.

"You're doing this because of paintings?! Six fucking paintings, Laurence, to pay for what you did to me! That warrants what you're doing to me now?!"

"Careful, Eve." Laurence opened the jacket of the gray double breasted suit he wore, and revealed a gun. "You wouldn't want to upset me while your *husband* is here next to me."

Pure hate coursed through Eve so violently she had to clench her fists and bite her cheek to keep from saying something that would cause Adam to get hurt.

"I will give you the paintings back."

"You think this is just about those fucking paintings? *Non, Eve, tu me dois tellement plus que cela.*"

She wanted to scream at him. How dare he say *she* owes *him*? After what he did to her, those paintings didn't even come close to repaying her for that.

"What do you want? Money? More paintings? I'll give you everything I have, just let Adam go and leave us alone."

"I told you what I wanted. I want you to lose everything the way I did."

Eve wasn't getting anywhere being antagonistic with him, but she didn't know how to separate the hatred she felt with what she needed to do. She didn't think anyone could be worse than Tony, but this man? This man that tore her apart, and worse, hurt her husband? There was a special place in hell for this man.

"I don't understand, Laurence. I took paintings, that's all."

"The photo," he said simply, as though she would understand his meaning.

Confusion settled on Eve's face. "I never showed that photo to anyone else." She glanced at Adam, who had murder in his eyes looking at Laurence. "I only gave that photo to you so that you would be motivated to do as I asked."

"It did not matter that you didn't use it against me, Eve. You gave it to me. My wife found it."

"You *kept* it?!" Why in the hell would he keep ... she shuddered when she thought of the answer.

"Because of you, my wife thought I was having an affair."

Eve scoffed. Certainly not the smartest thing to do in this situation, but she couldn't hold it back. She knew what that photo looked like. It was burned into her brain. How could anyone think that was consensual?

"Seriously? She thought that a seventeen year old girl would want to be brutalized by you? Was she crazy?"

Laurence's jaw twitched, as he fought to hold on to his control. "She left me and took my daughter."

"You can't possibly blame that on me! You should have been smart enough to destroy that photo!"

Laurence's face flushed with anger. He reached for the gun, and Eve thought of nothing but getting to Adam.

"No!" Eve ran the distance separating her and Adam, positioning herself in front of him. "You want to kill someone for your mistake, kill me! Adam did *nothing* wrong!"

"Eve, don't." Adam's voice pierced her heart. She would kill Laurence for the pain he put Adam in.

"Here I am, Laurence," she said, ignoring Adam's pleas. "Your wife left you because of me. You want me to pay for that, then kill *me*."

∞

An ugly smile marred Laurence's face. She didn't know they were alone. She had no clue that he had told those working for him that he wanted this for himself. He could tell her whatever he wanted, make her do whatever he wanted. Then, he would go after her daughter.

"No, I'm not going to kill you, Eve. At least not right now." He flicked his gaze up, and around as though he were looking at others. "I'm going to make you do what I had to do. You see, my wife came across your 'sob' story here in the States. Unfortunately, she recognized your face, only older now. The damn bitch looked you up, put two and two together and realized you were underage when the photo was taken. The greedy cunt asked for more money, or she would go to my business associates and the authorities claiming what a monster I was. Even went as far as to say that I would hurt my daughter."

∞

"*Oh, God. You killed her.*" Which meant, he wanted her to kill Adam. Not a chance. No matter what he threatened her with, she wouldn't do that.

"She gave me no choice. *You* gave me no choice." He pointed the gun at Eve, then glanced behind her at Adam. "I'm actually giving you a choice. Either you do it, or I will. Either way, you lose everything."

Oh, Adam, please forgive me for saying this, Eve begged silently. She looked at him briefly, trying to convey to him that she was only saying and doing what she needed for their survival. "I will still have Bella … and Lainey."

∞

Adam repeated over and over in his mind that Eve was his, and only his. She said these things to help them, not because that's how she felt. Did it hurt? Fuck yes. But, he had to keep focused. He had to find a way out of this. If anything happened to Eve, or if she were forced to hurt him, it would be devastating. Adam didn't think Eve would be able to come back from something like that. She has been strong, enduring so much that Adam found it amazing it all didn't bring her to her knees. However, if she had to do this, he was afraid it would be the one thing that breaks her. Adam continued what he had been doing since waking up here. He pulled on the plastic ties wrapped around his already bloody wrists with the little strength he had left. That son of a bitch had been zapping him with electricity just for the fucking fun of it. Adam would give anything to be able to put this fucker out of Eve's misery.

"No, Eve, you won't. Once we're done here, they're next."

That ugly, evil grin made Eve wish she had had Laurence killed after paying him a visit two years ago and making him hand over priceless paintings. God, she had wanted to. But, she wasn't like Tony. Eve was not a murderer. Oh, but if she got her hands on that gun, she would turn into one right now.

"You'll never find them," she said icily.

"You'll take me to them," he challenged.

Eve smiled, knowing it would piss him off. "I don't know where they are, Laurence. I put them on a plane before coming here. Destination unknown to me. You'll never get to them."

"Fucking bitch! I should have killed you that night."

Déjà vu, Eve thought mirthlessly. She remembered that night, right before he was killed, Maurice had said almost the same thing to her. How many lives did she have? Was she finally on her last one?

Chapter Nineteen

"Laurence! Put the gun down!"

The intense relief she felt almost floored Eve. She hadn't thought they would find her so soon, but then, she wasn't exactly sure how long she had been there.

"Fuck you! The bitch deserves to die!"

"That wasn't our agreement!"

Relief turned into pure shock, and Eve whirled around to stare at Billy. He wasn't in the instructions she left Lainey. Agreement? What the fuck? Her eyes darted from Billy to Adam, with Adam's expression mirroring her own shocked expression.

Adam locked eyes with Eve, not knowing how much longer they had. *I love you*, he mouthed.

Eve's face became a picture of unadulterated grief. She had failed. It was she most important task she had in her life, to save Adam, and she failed. *I love you, too*, she returned.

The entire exchange of glances and declarations of love took place in the matter of seconds. But, it felt as if time had stopped for them.

"I'm backing out of our agreement. I made the mistake of letting her live years ago. I won't make that mistake …"

It happened so fast, Eve didn't even have time to react. For the second time in as many weeks, she was covered with someone else's blood. Laurence's body is laying at her feet, blood from the hole in his head covering her sneakers.

"Beautiful? Look at me."

Eve's brow furrowed in confusion, but she brought her eyes up to meet Adam's.

"Focus, Eve. I'm here."

She had to cut him loose. Laurence was dead, and no one came after them. That must mean … she took a tentative step towards Adam.

"Don't." Billy's voice was low. It wasn't menacing, but it made her stop her advance.

Eve turned to Billy, slowly. "Billy?"

He looked a little shell-shocked himself, visibly shaking, but still holding his gun up. "It wasn't supposed to be this way."

"I don't understand, Billy."

Her voice was so soft, and sounded so young at that moment that all he wanted to do was go to her, and wrap her in his arms. "I lied to you before, Eve, darling. Eduardo did talk. He gave Laurence up almost immediately." He didn't tell her that he had offered him immunity. It wasn't in his authority to do so, but it got him what he wanted. And, now Eduardo was dead. The bastard tried to kill the woman Billy loved. There was no way he would've let him live.

Eve gasped. "You lied to me."

"I had to, my love. If I had told you, you would have gotten to Laurence before me. I needed to know why he was after you. You wouldn't have told me the truth." Billy's voice became harsh, scolding her.

Eve shook her head. She couldn't process any of this information, and it was frustrating her. All she wanted to do was get Adam out of that damn chair and get him checked out by a doctor.

"You're not making sense, Billy." She started towards Adam again. "Just help me get him loose, I need to get him to the hospital."

"I said stay away from him!" Billy's booming voice echoed throughout the empty warehouse.

Eve jerked her hand back, keeping her perplexed eyes on Adam. She saw him shake his head, the move so slight, she almost didn't notice. He face held such sorrow, she found it hard to stay on her feet, and not crumble before him. Then, Eve felt the anger rise in her like nothing she had ever felt before. She whipped around to face Billy.

"What the *fuck* is going on, Billy? By lying to me, you put my husband and my daughter in danger! How could you do that?!"

"I would never have allowed anything to happen to Bella, Eve. You must know that."

"And, Adam?"

"Eve, darling ..."

"Don't you dare! You were going to let Laurence kill my husband!"

"A necessity. He would have only stood in our way, trying to keep us apart."

Eve stared at him as if he had grown a second head. "You're delusional," she whispered.

Billy's eyes hardened. "You never even gave me a chance. I did everything I could for you, I helped you with Tony, I made that file implying you were a whore disappear, I …"

"*You* are married. *You* have children. *You* are a part of a past I want to forget!"

She stepped towards Billy, dismissing Adam's warnings to stop.

"I couldn't love you then, Billy, because I was a young girl who had just gone through the most horrible thing a girl could go through. As the years went by, I couldn't love you because you reminded me of that time, and I found Adam." Eve took another step. "I will *never* love you now because you have conspired to kill the love of my life."

She saw the hurt fill Billy's eyes, but didn't care. No matter how deep she looked inside herself, she would never be able to find compassion for him.

"You're just emotional right now. Once all of this is behind us …" His words trailed of in stunned silence as Eve grabbed his hand that held the gun and pressed it to her chest over her heart.

"Kill me, Billy."

"Eve!" Adam struggled against the ties, completely oblivious to the pain of them cutting into him. He had one thought. To get to Eve.

She focused on Billy, gripping his hand tightly when he tried to pull away.

"Kill me," she said again.

"I'm not going to kill you, Eve." Billy's voice was incredulous.

"But, you'll kill Adam?"

"I doubt he's going to let you divorce him without a fight. This is a solution."

Eve pushed the gun harder against her chest.

"Then you'll have to kill me, too. I won't live without him. I can't. And, I'll never be with you."

Eve's eyes, normally a light grey that affected him every time he saw her, turned as dark as a storm cloud. He saw it before she said the words.

"I hate you, William," she said icily.

"You don't mean that," he whispered.

"Oh, yes, I do. I hate you. And, if you hurt Adam, you better make sure you kill me, too. If you don't, I will kill you. I don't care if I have to spend the rest of my life in prison for it."

"Eve!"

Eve's stare never wavered, even as Charlie and James burst through the door, calling out her name. Vaguely, she was aware of an army of people filing in, surrounding them. Somewhere down deep she knew Lainey had followed her instructions, waiting until they were safe before contacting Captain Harris and James, and telling them to track her phone.

"What the hell is going on?" James trained his gun on Donovan, while Harris watched the scene intently.

"Get me out of this fucking chair!" Adam's roar bounced off the walls. Fuck, he needed to get to Eve before Donovan did what she told him to do.

The staring contest between Billy and Eve continued. She refused to flinch, still holding his wrist tightly. It was Billy that looked away first, tugging his hand away from her. He looked around in complete shock, see he was surrounded. This was not how this was supposed to happen! Laurence was going to kill Adam, and he would come in, save Eve and she would finally be with him. It was a flawless plan! That damned bastard screwed him and now Eve hated him. His heart broke looking at the woman in front of him.

Adam, finally free of his restraints, rushed to Eve, pushing her behind him. He could literally feel the rage pumping through his body, and it took every bit of strength to keep from going after Donovan. He felt Eve press her body to his, grasping his shirt to steady herself, and he reached behind him putting his hands firmly on her thighs.

"What is going on here, Agent Donovan?"

"He was working with that fucker Laurence," Adam answered when Donovan said nothing.

A sound of disbelief came from Harris, but James' sneer left no doubt that he believed it completely.

"Is this true, Billy?"

"I just told you …"

Eve squeezed Adam's bicep, and his mouth clamped closed. She preferred to let Donovan hang himself, so Adam would comply. Let the fucker hang, as long as he was out of their life for good.

Billy's dazed eyes darted around. He was trapped, he had lost the woman he had loved for most of his adult life, and when his family found out about this, he would lose them, too. He had nothing. Losing Eve alone left him with nothing.

"Drop the gun, Agent Donovan. This doesn't have to get any worse." Charlie's voice soothed, but Eve heard the underlying anger.

Billy's head jerked to Charlie. "Worse? *Worse?* She *hates* me!" He paced, unconcerned about the guns pointed at him. He waved the gun around, talking to himself, mumbling about how it should have been different. "She's supposed to be with me!"

Eve watched in fascination as the man she has known for years completely lost his mind. She wrapped her arms around Adam's waist, fully aware that Billy saw the gesture. She saw his eyes move to her hands that were clasped together, holding Adam close. And, when he looked in her eyes, she saw the defeat.

She couldn't say if she knew what he was going to do in that moment, but it didn't surprise her when he lifted his hands in surrender. It didn't shock her when, still watching her, he brought the gun below his chin and pulled the trigger.

Chapter Twenty

Adam leaned against the back of Eve's Lexus inside the hangar. He had been released from the hospital with a broken nose, cuts around the wrists where he had been bound, a broken rib and other minor injuries that he didn't think about now. What he thought about now was seeing his baby girl. And, wondering what it's going to be like seeing Lainey now that there were no doubts about what happened between her and Eve.

Eve paced in front of him, twirling her wedding rings around her finger, and Adam couldn't hold back the smile. He had never seen her so nervous. If he were being honest with himself, he'd admit he was happy she was so agitated. Maybe it was selfish, but he figured she owed him at least a bit of self-deprecation.

Eve glanced up at Adam and caught him staring at her with a sly grin.

"What?" Holy hell, she was nervous. While at the hospital, she and Adam didn't have a chance to talk about her affair with Lainey. Then, they were questioned by the police, and Eve found out Laurence's men had taken out Adam's security and took him at her warehouse. Most of Adam's wounds had come from fighting back, and trying to get away. When they got him strapped to the chair, that's when Laurence came in and started torturing Adam 'for the fun of it'. Hearing that had pissed Eve off enough to push out of her chair and walk out of Charlie's office. If she didn't get air, she would have gone crazy. And, though Adam held her hand on the way to the airport to pick up Bella, he stayed silent. She had wanted to ask him what he was thinking, but was too much of a coward.

"Nothing," was Adam's reply, but kept his grin.

Well, he wasn't glaring at her, so that was a plus. She looked at her wrist, rolled her eyes then went to Adam and checked his watch. They had another fifteen minutes or so before Bella—and Lainey—got here. No time like the present, she thought with a deep breath.

"Talk to me, *amant*."

His grin faltered. This wasn't something he wanted to talk about, but he supposed it was inevitable. "What would you like me to say, Eve?"

"I don't know! What are you thinking? How do you feel?" Her heart hammered painfully in her chest. He had said he forgave her, but she couldn't be certain that he didn't just say that because of the situation they were in. Maybe he thought they weren't going to make it out alive, and wanted her to think everything was okay.

He studied her, and his own feelings, in silence. Adam could see her elevated pulse in the vein on her long, elegant neck. "I'm not sure how to feel," he answered honestly.

Eve closed her eyes. She couldn't blame him, really. When she had thought he had been with another woman, she was furious, and he hadn't done anything wrong. She *slept* with Lainey. She opened her eyes, focusing on Adam again.

"Yell at me. Tell me you hate me. Do *something*!"

When he said nothing, she dragged a frustrated hand through her hair. Eve was about to turn away when Adam grabbed her waist and pulled her crashing into him. He crushed his mouth to hers in a mind-blowing, breath-taking, knee-weakening kiss. She was panting by the time he broke the kiss.

"I don't want to yell at you," he said softly. "I don't hate you. I think I have to wait until I see ... Lainey and then assess what I feel."

She heard the hesitation at Lainey's name, and sighed. That was not a good sign. The kiss on the other hand, that gave her hope. Eve brushed her hands up his chest, wrapping her arms around his neck. Depending on his answer to the question she was about to ask, she may need to hold on. A thrill went through her when he reciprocated by wrapping his arms around her waist, spreading his legs so she fit between them.

"Baby? Do you ... would you ..." Eve lowered her head and squeezed her eyes shut. God, it hurt her so much to have to ask this. When she looked up at Adam again, tears filled her eyes. "Do you want me to stop being Lainey's friend?"

The words tumbled out of her rapidly, and Adam watched as a tear escaped, sliding down her smooth cheek. It broke his heart.

"That was really hard for you, wasn't it? Asking me that."

She nodded, unable to trust her voice, and Adam sighed. He reached up and took a strand of her hair between his thumb and forefinger. "Could you do that?" he asked gently. "*Would* you do that for me?"

Eve's face was the definition of mourning, and Adam watched as more tears fell. But, she nodded. He pressed his forehead to hers, and asked what he needed to know.

"Why, Eve? Why did you sleep with her? Tell me what she means to you."

"Adam ..."

His arms tightened around her, urging her to continue.

"I felt a connection with Lainey from the moment I met her. I can't explain it. Believe me, I've tried explaining it to myself, but she's the best friend I've ever had," she said softly. "No one had ever wanted to get to know *me*. No one ever saw past the façade enough to know there was more there." She saw his eyes lower, and brought a hand to his chin to lift it. "Except you and Lainey."

"But, it was her that helped you. Not me."

"That's not true, *amant*. You had already begun getting in here." Eve placed a hand over her heart before returning it around the back of his neck. "But, she made me feel ... safe."

"I don't?"

"Oh, baby, that's not ... I didn't ... that's not how I meant it. Of course you make me feel safe. What I meant to say was she was safe for me. I feared nothing with her."

"Because she's a woman?"

"Because she's Lainey," Eve responded quietly. "Maybe the fact that she was a woman played into it, thinking about what happened to me." She tilted her head and studied him. "You haven't asked the one question I thought you would ask."

A small smile played at his lips. "You think I should be asking if you're a lesbian? Or, at the least, bisexual?"

"It would be normal for you to ask, I guess."

Adam chuckled. "One thing I do know about you, beautiful, is you're not a lesbian. You wouldn't be able to make love to me the way that you do if you were." His brows furrowed as he analyzed her. "I don't think you ..." he cleared his throat and tried again. "I don't think it had anything to do with gender. It was just how you felt."

Eve gave him a small smile. He understood her. Always had. And, she rewarded that by hurting him. "You're being extremely understanding about this," she said warily.

"Like I said, beautiful, I can't be sure how I'm going to feel when the plane gets here. But, I'm trying to understand your side of it. I can't tell you it doesn't hurt like fuck knowing you slept with someone else." He saw her flinch, and tightened his grip. "Can I get back to you on your question?"

Eve knew he was talking about her question about her friendship with Lainey, and felt sick to her stomach. She had no idea if she could survive without Lainey, but whatever Adam decided she would honor. So, she nodded.

"And, if I ask you to stop being her friend?"

Eve sucked in a shaky breath, that literally hurt her heart. "I would be devastated if I lost Lainey," she answered honestly. "But, I couldn't live without you."

Adam stared at her, taking in the enormity of her words. Before he could answer, they heard the engine of the plane as it taxied to the hangar. He felt Eve stiffen in his arms, saw the fear and nervousness in her eyes, and he kissed her gently on the lips before letting her go.

Eve turned to watch the approach of the private jet, fighting against the anxiety that threatened to take over. How would she act around Lainey? What could she say or do that wouldn't upset Adam—or Lainey? The answer was nothing, she thought miserably. Bella is home. Focus on that, Eve.

Chapter Twenty-One

Lainey stepped out on the stairs with Bella in her arms, and Eve's eyes lit up seeing her baby girl. She focused squarely on Bella, waiting a bit impatiently for them to get to her. Finally, they closed the distance and Eve couldn't hold back any longer.

Eve plucked Bella out of Lainey's arms, barely sparing her a glance, and Lainey felt that in her soul.

"There's momma's baby girl." Eve hugged Bella tightly to her chest, fighting back tears. She kissed her baby's face, not wanting to let go ever again. She felt Adam come up behind her and Eve finally relented, handing Bella over to her daddy. Slowly, she turned to Lainey. The pain was so intense, Eve didn't know how she was able to stay standing.

"*Thank you*," she whispered to Lainey giving her a quick one arm hug. Eve gave Jack a quick kiss on the cheek, thanking him, and then turned her attention to Kevin and Darren. "That wasn't a very long vacation, was it?" She hoped her voice sounded light, and she forced a smile to her face.

"Nope, but Cap'n Steve let us each fly!" Darren gave Eve a toothy grin, full of enthusiasm that only a child oblivious to the drama around him can have.

"That sounds fun." Eve caught Kevin's intense stare jumping between her and Adam. She remembered that Adam had bruises and a bandage across his nose, and thought about how confusing and upsetting that could be for the boys. She kissed Darren on the cheek, then bent to hug Kevin. *"Everything is okay."* She took his face in her hands, holding his gaze. When he nodded slightly, she let go.

Adam watched the exchange between Eve and the entire Stanton family. It wasn't just Lainey she loved. Would he be able to take her away from all of them? He noticed Lainey's attention on him, and ordered his body to move to her.

"Thank you for taking care of Bella," he told her quietly, offering her a quick—and somewhat uncomfortable—kiss on the cheek. He turned to Jack giving him a hearty handshake and a nod. Adam gave both of the boys a grin and a fist bump before going back to Eve, and wrapping a protective—and perhaps possessive—arm around her.

"Eve and I would like to invite you over for dinner to thank you properly for what you did for us."

Eve barely stopped the surprise from showing on her face. He hadn't mentioned this to her, and honestly, she didn't think he would want Lainey to be around.

"Are you sure you don't want to just relax together?" Lainey asked tentatively. Something was definitely wrong, but she couldn't for the life of her figure out what it was. Maybe it was just the stress of everything they went through. She was hoping Eve would tell her everything, but Eve wouldn't even look at her.

"We have the rest of our lives to relax together, Lainey." Damn it all if he couldn't keep the bitterness out of his voice. "Right now, we would like you to come over." He looked pointedly over at Jack for back up.

"We would be honored," Jack answered before Lainey could say anything more.

"Why did you do that?"

They were driving back to the house after making plans to meet the Stantons there in two hours. Eve had been quiet for the first few minutes of the drive, but couldn't hold it in anymore.

Adam glanced at Eve. "Why not?"

"You know why not, *amant*."

"Eve, when Lainey stepped off that plane I felt anger." He couldn't miss Eve's quietly sad sigh. "I need more time with her to figure this out. To see if I can deal with this."

Eve bowed her head, unwilling to let Adam see the hopelessness she felt. He didn't deserve that. But, she did. She was the one that hurt him, and although the mere thought of losing Lainey depressed Eve immensely, she would do as Adam asks if it meant saving her marriage.

Lainey studied Eve from inside the house. Adam, Jack and the boys were out by the grill, and though he looked tired and battered, Adam had seemed okay. Eve, on the other hand, seemed ... broken. She was leaning on the railing of the back porch, shoulders slumped, head down. Lainey couldn't imagine what she had been through—especially since she still hasn't heard the story. Whatever it was had caused a complete shift in Eve. Unable to stay away any longer, Lainey went to her.

"Eve?" She saw Eve flinch, but change her posture to stand straighter. Lainey's heart broke a little more. Eve was putting on a façade for her.

Eve didn't turn to Lainey, but granted her a quick glance. It hurt too much to look at her. "Hi."

Lainey leaned on the railing with her, tentatively reaching over to place her hand on Eve's. She could be imagining things because of the tension she felt, but she could swear Eve stiffened in response to her touch. More, Eve looked ... afraid, looking quickly at Adam before pulling away. Lainey followed Eve's eyes, and saw Adam watching them intently.

"Honey ..." Was that a whimper she heard from Eve? Lainey quickly checked on Bella who was quietly, and happily, playing on her blanket. If it wasn't Bella, it had to be Eve. "Talk to me, Eve."

God, the pain was almost overwhelming. How was she going to make it through this? After everything else that has happened to her, this is the thing that brings her down? It made Eve fear that Laurence would get what he wanted all along.

Just when Lainey thought Eve wouldn't say anything, she spoke in barely a whisper.

"*He knows.*"

"Sorry?"

Eve took a breath, and tried again. "Adam knows, Lainey."

"Knows what?"

"About us."

A sharp gasp filled the air around them as Lainey tried to comprehend the ramifications of what Eve told her.

"H-how? W-why would you tell him?" Oh God! Jack! Adam is down there with Jack and her sons. He's going to tell them!

"I didn't. He already knew." Another glance at Lainey told Eve what Lainey feared. It wasn't losing Eve, it was Adam telling her husband. "He's not going to tell him," she said icily.

Lainey's eyes snapped back to Eve. Why on earth was she mad at her? Did Eve blame her for this? She hadn't been the only one to pursue the relationship.

"You're mad at *me*?"

"Forget it. Perhaps you just made this easier."

"Made what easier?"

"Saying goodbye to you."

Lainey gripped the railing in a white-knuckled grip. She felt all of the air leave her in an instant. She hadn't thought of the possibility of Eve saying goodbye to her, because she didn't think Eve could do it anymore than Lainey could. Hearing the coldness in Eve's voice only made it worse.

Eve watched the blood drain from Lainey's face, saw the death grip she had on the railing as if she would crumble if she let go, and immediately regretted her harsh words. She had been completely wrong, and she couldn't wrap her arms around Lainey to show her how sorry she was. "I'm sorry I said that."

Through her own painfully thundering heartbeat pounding in her ears, she heard Eve's pain and sincerity.

"Are you saying goodbye to me?"

A tear rolled down Eve's cheek, followed by another. "That's up to Adam," she answered miserably.

Adam couldn't concentrate on what Jack and the boys were saying. His eyes stayed trained on Eve and Lainey, watching the exchange. And, he was staggered by the tremendous grief he saw in each woman. Hell, he could feel it.

"Excuse me, Jack. I hate to leave you out here to cook, but I have to speak with Lainey for a bit."

Jack cast a curious glance at Adam, then back at his wife and Eve. Something was definitely wrong. Why did Adam need to speak with Lainey?

"Lainey?"

"Eve is going through a lot right now. I just want to make sure Lainey understands what's going on."

"Ah. Right."

Adam didn't wait for more dialogue, instead he made his way back to the house. Fuck. He could see the fear in Eve's eyes as he approached, and hated it.

"Can I speak with you?"

It took Lainey a few seconds to recognize that Adam was talking to her. She took a step back from him, bumping into the rail with her hip.

"I would never hurt you, Lainey," he said softly, seeing her apprehension for going anywhere with him. "But, I think we need to talk alone."

"Adam …" Eve didn't want Adam saying anything to Lainey that would hurt her more.

"Alone, Eve."

"It's fine," Lainey cut in before Eve could object again. "I owe him at least that much."

Lainey followed Adam inside, grabbing her purse as they made their way to the office. Once they were closed in, she waited.

Adam took a steadying breath before turning to face Lainey. "I hate what you did."

Lainey lowered her eyes and nodded. When he said nothing else, she looked up at him and saw he was waiting for her to say something. She chose her words carefully and honestly. "I can't regret what I did, Adam, but I do regret hurting you. I care so much about you, and it kills me to see you and Eve hurting."

"But, you wouldn't change it?"

Lainey shook her head.

"Are you in love with my wife?"

Lainey hesitated, shutting her eyes briefly. "I love Eve. I can't deny that. But, we both made our decisions, Adam, and I chose Jack. Because, I'm *in* love with him."

Adam pulled a hand through his hair and began pacing. This would be so much easier if he didn't care for Lainey. "How do I live with this? How can I allow you to be in my house, with my wife, knowing what I know?" He made a noise of frustration. "You helped me."

Lainey frowned in confusion.

"When Eve and I were going through our problems, you told me not to give up. *You* told me to open my eyes. You were sleeping with her then, right?"

An embarrassed flush crept up Lainey's neck. It was the only answer Adam needed.

"Why did you help me?"

"Because I knew you and Eve belonged together," Lainey said simply. "What I had with her, I couldn't stop if I tried. And, believe me, I tried, Adam. It was something we both needed, which is why I can't regret it. But, oh God, I never wanted to hurt you." She took a step closer to Adam. "She believed she didn't deserve you. That you needed someone better, that could give you more."

"There is no one better," Adam muttered. Even now, after everything he knew, he still believed that.

"If she hadn't felt that way, I doubt she could've been with me." The admission hurt her, but she knew deep down it was true.

Adam softened. "She needs you."

"She needs us. I've never seen her like this. But, she told me it's up to you if she says goodbye to me."

Adam blinked in surprise. Eve was serious. She would give Lainey up for him. Knowing that was more powerful than anything. "You're right. She needs us. But, damn it, Lainey, I have to be able to trust both of you."

Here goes. "Adam, she knew I was having those deeper feelings again. She's the one who couldn't do anything about it. She wouldn't do that to you. And, despite what I just said, I couldn't do that to Jack or you. I know it's going to be difficult to trust me, but I promise you, Eve will not jeopardize her relationship with you."

"I wish I could believe that." He was beginning to get a throbbing headache. Sitting down and relaxing was probably the thing he should be doing, yet he's here confronting his wife's … what? Best friend? Former lover?

Lainey turned to her purse, digging around the enormous thing until she found what she was looking for.

"Before you make any judgments, please read these. I found them in Bella's diaper bag. I probably shouldn't have read the one addressed to me, but I did. I didn't read yours or Bella's."

Adam narrowed his eyes, studying the three envelopes in Lainey's hand. His, Bella's and Lainey's names were written in Eve's unmistakable handwriting. When Lainey pushed them closer to him, he took them. Instinctively, he thrust Lainey's back to her.

She pushed it back to him. "Read it."

Chapter Twenty-Two

Eve sat alone in her studio, staring at the canvas in front of her. Adam was making her sweat with his decision about Lainey. He had been civil enough, even to Lainey, during dinner, but he still hasn't said anything to her.

When Lainey and her family left, Eve waited patiently for Adam to come to her. Instead, he locked himself away in the office after they put an exhausted Bella to bed. With a broken heart, Eve came out to her studio. And, nothing. The aroma of canvases and paints did nothing to inspire her. She literally felt as though all of the talent she once possessed had just disappeared.

Eve unlocked the back room, forcing herself to go in. Everything in that room reminded her of the most inspired time in her life. After she met Lainey and began opening her heart, creativity flowed through her like never before. Some of her best work was in this room. Including the portraits of both Adam and Lainey. She wanted this back.

"Eve?"

Eve gasped, stumbling into some of the paintings leaning against the wall.

"You shouldn't be here. Please, Lainey, you have to leave. If Adam finds you here …"

"I asked her to come, Eve." Adam stepped inside and stood next to Lainey.

Her head was spinning. This was it. He was going to tell her his decision now. Did he bring Lainey here to say goodbye? She didn't want to know. If he didn't say the words, she could pretend everything was the way it was before.

"Eve …"

"Stop! I can't … I'm sorry."

She ran past them, out of the studio, across the lawn and into the garage. She blindly grabbed her keys off their hook and slipped behind the wheel of her Jag. It roared to life, drowning out Adam and Lainey's shouts. She had to get out of there. Somewhere deep down she hated herself for being so weak and running instead of facing her problems, but she felt so completely unbalanced. She honestly didn't know if she could deal with this. At least not now. Not so soon after what they had just been through. She has had enough. Her entire life it's been one thing after another, and she has had enough.

∞

"Let me go up first." Adam parked next to Eve's Jag in the garage of her gallery. He turned to Lainey and placed a hand on hers. "She's not going to like this, you know."

"I know." Lainey was nervous. She took the time waiting for her parents to come over to Eve's to watch Bella, and driving into the city to try to come up with the right words to say to Eve. "This is what's best, right?"

Adam nodded. He was sure this was right, but that didn't mean it would be easy for Eve to accept.

Lainey sighed. "Okay. Text me when you're ready for me to come up."

"Just give me five minutes, then make your way up. She'll need to see you."

She touched his forearm to stop him as he started to get out of the car. "Adam ..."

He shook his head.

∞

He found Eve sitting in a corner, staring at Lainey's display. She had kept it in tact, having Lainey make only minor changes here and there, since the re-opening of the gallery. Damn, she looked so young and scared, hugging her legs and resting her chin on her knees. She had been crying, and the sight ruined him. He knelt in front of her, noting that it took a few seconds for her to focus on him.

"Eve, beautiful, are you okay?" His heart plummeted when she shook her head weakly. "Did you run because you were afraid to hear what I had to say?"

Eve nodded, still saying nothing.

"I won't take her away from you, baby," he told her softly, and she looked up at him, a small spark of hope forming in her eyes. "I can't do that to you, or to us. I need to trust you and Lainey. I think I can do that."

Eve frowned in confusion. "*You can?*"

"He knows I would never do anything to jeopardize your love for each other," Lainey said quietly, stooping beside Adam and placing a hand on her arm.

Eve stiffened, looking to Adam for any sign of anger. When she saw nothing but compassion, she relaxed.

"What changed?" Eve's voice was hoarse from crying, and she winced from the sound.

Adam reached behind him, taking envelopes out of his pocket. Eve's eyes widened when she saw what they were.

"You read them?!" She looked over at Lainey. Betrayal neared the surface, but she just didn't have the strength to let it through. She closed her eyes again, laying her chin back on her knees.

Adam caught Lainey's attention. They made a non-verbal agreement that this was not the time to approach Eve with what they thought she needed.

"Baby, you're exhausted and you've been through hell. Let's go home." Eve looked up at him again, then over to Lainey. "Lainey will drive you home in the Jag, and I'll follow."

Once again, surprise flickered in her eyes.

"I told you, beautiful, I'm not taking her from you. We'll discuss it more later, but I need you to understand that I'm trusting you."

A tear escaped, much to Eve's dismay. He's not making her give Lainey up. She didn't deserve him, but she thanked God for him.

Adam stood, holding his hand out to Eve. She grasped it, and he lifted her to her feet. "I care for Lainey, too, baby," he said close to her ear. "I know she wants the best for you, as do I. We'll get through this. I promise."

They walked down to the garage, and Adam deposited Eve into the passenger seat of her Jaguar. He reached in and strapped the seatbelt around her, then squeezed Lainey's hand before kissing Eve's lips gently.

"I'll see you at home."

He closed her in, knowing she was in good hands. Lainey wouldn't let anything happen to her, and after their talk and the letters, he knew he could trust them both.

Eve would spend the rest of her life showing Adam and Bella that she deserves them and their trust. Knowing that Lainey would be there to help her, only strengthened that resolve. She didn't know how she could ever thank both Adam and Lainey for being there for her throughout the most difficult times of her life, but she was glad she was going to have the chance to figure it out.

Inspiration will return, she was sure of it. She didn't know when, or if this sadness that was so deep down she didn't know how to get to it, would go away. But, she was ready to focus on a drama free—or at least murder free—life with the people she loved the most.

Epilogue

Seven months later ...

"Eve, honey? Where do you want this?"

Eve turned to where Lainey held up a creative sculpture from a local artist. The lines and curves gave the piece a sexy feel to it, and Eve liked it.

"I think up front so that it's one of the first sculptures to be seen. Perhaps next to the 'Evolution of Eve'." She grinned, as always, when she thought of that sculpture. Why not? She felt as though she has been through an evolution of her own. Here she was in California, with Lainey, setting up her new gallery. Adam would be there in a few hours to put finishing touches to the main display area, as well as making sure everything else was just perfect.

On a good day, she could put everything that happened with Laurence and Billy out of her mind, and pretend it never happened. She didn't always have a good day, but it was getting easier. Eve glanced up towards the offices, knowing Bella was up there with Lexie, and smiled. Yes, it was getting easier. She had a lot to be happy about these days, and she was determined to do just that.

"Good morning!" Blaise waltzed in bearing gifts of Ellie's coffee and croissants. Eve decided then that Blaise was definitely someone she liked. "Oh, wow! It's starting to look so amazing in here!"

Eve took the coffee that Blaise held out to her. "Thank you."

Lainey joined them, graciously accepting the to-go cup from Blaise. "There are so many talented artists here in LA," she commented, looking around the gallery that held similarities to the one in New York, but also had its own flair. It was Eve's way of having any type of continuity in her life. Lainey had always wondered about the reasoning for that, but never got around to asking Eve. Maybe one day. "Including you, Blaise. Your flower arrangements are amazing."

Blaise offered a shy smile. "Thank you. It's always easier to be creative when you love what you do. I'm sure you both understand that."

"Hmm." Eve took a sip of her coffee in lieu of replying. She figured it wasn't something Blaise necessarily wanted a response to, so she changed the subject. "How are things with Mr. Steele?"

"Ugh, the man is infuriating!"

Eve and Lainey exchanged a look before laughing.

"Men can certainly be infuriating. Especially …"

"Stop right there," Blaise warned Lainey. "I get enough of that from Ellie." She popped a piece of croissant into her mouth, hiding her slightly annoyed grin. "Your flowers for the opening are going to be beautiful."

"Nice segue," Eve teased. "But, I'm excited to see them."

"Are you sure you don't want to see what I'm doing first?"

"I'm sure. I've seen enough of your work to know they'll be perfect."

Blaise beamed at her. "Well, I thank you. And, on that note, I suppose I need to get to the shop. Keep up the great work!" She called as she walked out. Blaise waved through the front window, causing Lainey and Eve to smile.

"She's nice."

"Mmhmm." Eve moved to the display Lainey had finished earlier. It was as magnificent as the one in New York, and Eve—no matter how much she fought it—felt a pang of jealousy. *Damn it.*

"Eve ..."

"I don't want to talk about it, Lainey. Please?"

"Okay, honey. That's fine. But, you know I'm here if you need me."

"I know." Eve gave her a small smile. "I'm glad you are here. I couldn't imagine doing this without you."

Lainey grinned. "I hope not. Mikey, by the way, is still a little miffed that he couldn't be here."

"Someone needed to run the gallery back home. He'll get over it."

Eve winked at her, and Lainey's heart smiled. Eve had kept herself guarded since what happened, allowing only a small amount of emotion, or even playfulness, to show. Unless she was with Bella, Eve rarely showed that carefree side. Both Adam and Lainey missed it greatly.

"I'm sure he will, but I bet he would've like to be here for the opening."

"Well, I hope so, since I'm flying him and his mother out for the event."

"Oh, Eve! That's wonderful! He's going to be so excited!"

Eve lifted a shoulder as though it wasn't a big deal, but she really did hope he would be excited. He had been a trooper throughout this whole ordeal, Eve figured he deserved at least this much. Her phone rang, interrupting her thoughts, and she grinned at the ringtone.

"Hello, *amant*."

Adam didn't even try to hold back the groan that stemmed from hearing her sexy voice. They had been apart for four days since he had to fly back to New York to take care of things at his own office. He missed her like crazy.

"Hey, beautiful. I just landed, so I'm on my way."

"You're here?" Eve's grin grew into a full-fledged, mega-watt, totally Eve smile. "Finally."

Adam cleared his throat, shifting in his seat in the back of the town car. He could imagine her smile, hear her sensuous voice that dropped an octave when she spoke to him, and knew whatever she was wearing—which was probably jeans since she was setting up the gallery, and his favorite—she looked amazing. He couldn't wait to get to her.

"How's our baby girl?"

Eve chuckled at Adam's obvious change of subject. "She's perfect as always. Lexie is teaching her about the sounds that animals make today. Wait until you hear her 'moo'."

Adam laughed. "Moo, huh? I can't wait. How's Lainey?"

Eve loved him for thinking to ask about Lainey. She knew he forgave her completely for her affair, and forgave Lainey, as well, but he didn't have to ask about her. That he did meant so much to her. "She's well. She's standing here wondering where to put a particularly explicit sculpture and blushing."

Eve burst out laughing when Lainey gave her the finger. She couldn't know that both Adam and Lainey cherished that sound, hoping that one day very soon, Eve would be laughing like that more often.

"Well, I'll be there in a little while," Adam told her, laughter ringing in his voice. "Tell her I'll give her a hand."

"You just want to see the particularly explicit sculpture," Eve teased.

"It has been four days since I've seen my wife. I may be a little ... ready for particularly explicit."

Eve turned away from Lainey, walking far enough away that she had privacy. "I'm ready for that, too, *amant*. Very much so."

"I missed you, baby."

"I missed you, too, gorgeous."

∞

Lainey caught a slight flush creep up Eve's neck, and she knew that this part of the conversation was a private moment between a husband and a wife. With a knowing smile, Lainey turned away and gave them their moment.

Eve Sumptor-Riley—Session One

"How are you today, Eve?"

I studied the woman in front of me. Poised. That's probably the first word that came to my mind when I first saw her. She had to be in her mid-fifties, well-groomed with warm chestnut hair that sparkled with a touch of gray. When I did my background check, I found that Dr. Willamena Woodrow has been a psychiatrist for more than twenty-five years, with a degree from the prestigious Johns Hopkins University. She had a soothing voice, but it still aggravated me. It's not her fault, really. I just don't want to be here.

"I'm fine."

She smiled, a nice, understanding smile. "You realize we have an hour together? It may be helpful if you were more elaborate with your answers."

I felt the corners of my mouth twitch for the first time since walking in this office. That actually made me like her a little more.

"I'm actually not sure what to say."

"Why don't you start with why you're here."

I laughed. "Because my husband and best friend thought I needed to talk to someone."

"You don't think you do?"

I watched her twirl her pen in her fingers, but noticed she still hasn't written anything down. Of course, I haven't said much.

"I've done well enough on my own so far," I answered.

"Hmm." This time she did write something, and then picked up a stack of papers to her right. "I've read your story, Eve. Anyone would have a difficult time in your situation. It isn't uncommon to seek someone to talk to."

"I'm not used to seeking anyone out."

"Maybe it's time you do."

Whether it was time or not, I didn't feel I had much choice. Adam and Lainey bombarded me with this request, practically giving me no choice but to agree.

Dr. Woodrow watched me silently, patiently, but when I still said nothing, she sighed. "Have you started painting again?"

The question made me wince, and wish that I hadn't disclosed that bit of information to her in the preliminary interview.

"No."

"Why do you think that is?"

I couldn't bite back the sigh. How the hell should I know why I couldn't paint. My relationship with Adam is strong again. My friendship with Lainey is wonderful. Even Adam and Lainey's relationship was mending. So why can't I paint?

"I don't know." My voice sounded smaller than I would have liked, but not being able to paint is killing me.

"Then, let me help you find that out," she said softly.

"I've survived a lot in my life. I just don't understand why I can't get past this."

"You may have survived, but are you certain that you've gotten over your past, Eve?"

I thought about her question. Okay, yes, I've had moments when the past catches up with me, but mostly I'm fine. I think.

"No." My answered surprised me. I opened my mouth to say yes, so why isn't that what came out?

"Then we should start there. In fact, why don't we start with your childhood."

I honestly tried to stifle the snicker at how clichéd that sounded to me.

Dr. Woodrow's expression held the tiniest bit of disapproval at my laughter. I didn't think psychiatrists were allowed to show emotion, however, that she did, made me trust her a little more.

"Where should I start?"

"What's the first thing that comes to your mind?"

I closed my eyes and thought back to things I wanted to forget. The first image that popped into my head was of my mother, bloodied and crying, huddled in the closet with me. She would rock me, whispering that everything would be okay, and I would believe her. Until it happened again and again. Eventually I stopped believing her, even resenting her more and more each time we huddled in that closet.

"*Help me forgive my mother.*" My voice was barely a whisper, and the words that were said brought tears to my eyes. I had no idea I still harbored feelings of blame for my mother. My love for her had always overshadowed everything else.

Well, hell. I guess there is something to this shrink business after all. I'm glad I'm rich. With as many things as I have gone through, it's going to take many, many hours to get through them all.

Be sure to follow Eve's therapy sessions online at:
http://blog.jourdynkelly.com/
to see how Eve copes with coming to terms
with everything that has happened to her.

Acknowledgements

This is my third book, and I have come to realize that I rely on the same people to give me honesty. What that tells me, is that I have a small core of people that I trust dearly.

Again, my family shows me that they believe in me without fail. Mom and Dad, you are always in my corner, and your continuous pride keeps me feeling like I can do anything. Kayla, your opinions are far more mature than your twenty-two years of age! I appreciate your honesty. Ty, I believe in you and your talent! Go for it! Thank you and Kayla for your support. Amber, you've come so far, and I'm so proud of you. Thank you for being on my side. Chelsea and Terry, your support is greatly appreciated (and I will get to the next Destined now, Chelsea!).

Daisy, once again I thank you for your patience with my sometimes incessant writing and obsessing over these characters. Your support and opinions are important to me, especially since you never pull any punches. Thank you!

Wanda and Sherry! You ladies gave me wonderful feedback on Flawed Perfection! I love that you love Eve as much as I do. Your honest opinions on Flawed Perfection helped me tremendously, and for that I thank you from the bottom of my heart!

Angela McLaurin (Fictional Formats), I couldn't be happier that I found such a talented formatter! You've made my books beautiful! Having a book that's as appealing to the eye as it is to the brain is so important. Thank you for all you do.

To my readers. Eve Sumptor (Riley) has been my favorite character to write. I couldn't let her go, which is why you will still find her online in her own words. I don't know where these therapy sessions will take Eve, but I hope you'll tune in to see her progress! Thank you all for reading and letting Eve, Adam, Lainey and Bella in your life. I hope to see you again for Blaise Knight's story!

About the Author

Jourdyn Kelly currently resides in Houston, Texas, writing novels and designing websites. Jourdyn has always enjoyed the arts in one form or another. Having completed her third novel, she believes that her love of writing comes from the fact that she loves to read. She was captivated by books that led you into different and exotic places and through impossible scenarios, letting you become someone else for a time. As she read, she was inspired to write herself and bring the characters in her mind to paper. She hopes that her writing will inspire others, or give them a way to escape from everyday life.

Jourdyn has spent her time working in a different area of the arts. As web designer, etc. for singer/actress Deborah Gibson, Jourdyn has had the opportunity to be involved in wonderful experiences, travel around the country and meet exciting people. Jourdyn believes this has helped with creating unique and lovable characters.

Other than writing Jourdyn spends her time caring for what she equates to as a zoo with 3 dogs, 2 cats, a bearded dragon, 3 frogs and 3 turtles. In the recent years, she has changed her lifestyle to include working out and eating right. She now competes in triathlons, has run her first half-marathon, and loves Muay Thai kickboxing, boxing and Krav Maga.

Jourdyn is presently working on the follow up to *Destined to Kill*.

Connect with Jourdyn Kelly online:

My Website:
http://www.jourdynkelly.com

Twitter:
https://twitter.com/JourdynK

Goodreads:
www.goodreads.com/author/show/2980644.Jourdyn_Kelly

Facebook:
https://www.facebook.com/AuthorJourdynKelly

Made in the USA
Columbia, SC
10 July 2024